Grandmas of the World, Rejoice!

What are Grandmas *really* made of? Sugar and Spice and All Things Sickeningly Nice, or Problems and Peeves that No One Believes? GRANDMA STRIKES BACK presents some impressive answers to this basic question. The premise is simple: being a grandparent is not just doing what comes naturally. It's a psychological state of being, like adolescence and old age, and it takes just as much painful, personal adjustment.

Edwina Sherudi contends that the weight of the Grandparent Legend has effectively kept many disappointed, disillusioned grandparents from expressing their views. In GRANDMA STRIKES BACK, she speaks out loudly and hilariously against the stereotype of grandmothers as people in their dotage, unfailingly sweet and endlessly devoted to the darling grandkids.

Yes, Grandma, there *is* more to life than babysitting and baking chocolate chip cookies!

GRANDMA
STRIKES
BACK

Edwina Sherudi

LEISURE BOOKS ∞ NEW YORK CITY

A LEISURE BOOK

Published by

Nordon Publications, Inc.
Two Park Avenue
New York, N.Y. 10016

To My Husband:

Who held my hand but not my mouth

Open rebuke is better than secret love. . .

Proverbs

Foreword

THIS book is not, and was never intended to be a textbook on grandparenthood. It is simply one grandma's personal account, written in blood, sweat, tears and laughter.

If you are one of those fortunate few who have walked in unmitigated joy through the thorny rose-bush path that leads to grandparenthood, please put this down and read no further. If, however, you are one of the vast majority who stop to wonder from time to time in the midst of the never-ending struggles that characterize this way of life, please come into my book, and let us commiserate together.

E.S.

Contents

GRANDMA
STRIKES BACK

Chapter I

GO TELL IT ON THE MOUNTAIN

THERE is nothing in life that prepares one for grandparenthood—which is neither grand nor parental. There may be enough cookbook material in the parenthood area to cover every possibility along that way, from the first skipped menstrual period to the grave, but the realm of grandparenthood is as uncharted as Jupiter or Mars.

Myths, of course, abound. Grandparents are unfailingly sweet, doting and dumb. They exist, like Whistler's Mother, in perennial lap positions, the better to hold little children and spoil them. Functionally, they care, they comfort, they tell stories, they babysit, and they exude an uncontrollable, unreasoning, unceasing pride in their condition, as if they not only invented the process, but also held exclusive rights to it. In short, any resemblance between grandparents and intelligent human beings who have raised whole families on their own and run households and pursued business or professional careers is purely coincidental.

So much for fantasy.

The truth about grandparenthood, unfortunately, is less easy to come by. Of such power is the weight of legend which surrounds the whole concept that even to question any of it—much less quibble with it—is to risk unleashing the kind of moralistic outrage previous generations used to reserve for deviant social behavior such as homosexuality. With the consequence that many disillusioned grandparents, never realizing that they are not unique or "unnatural" and that there is a vast conspiracy of silence, fit themselves into the sociological roles in which they find themselves cast with the whole-hearted professionalism of a Barbra Streisand on stage..

As did I.

When, for example, in my early grandparent days, people would respond to my announcement that my daughter, Debbie, was going to have a baby, with the customary Isn't-That-Wonderful, I never dared to ask why. Instead, so consistent was the exclamation—almost as if it were a recording, like the Weather Lady on the phone—and so enthusiastic, that instinctively I would grab at my brightest smile and hurriedly affirm, "Yes. Isn't it wonderful!"

When, similarly, there would be the next inevitable, "So You're - Going - To - Be - A - Grandmother - How - Exciting!" routine, intoned with all the gusto of a headliner emcee announcing the winner in a Miss America contest, I again never questioned the premise. Only to my husband did I dare to voice the secret, sacrilegious doubts that even then were beginning to emerge.

"By why is it wonderful?" I demanded this of Tim one night when we were getting ready for bed. "Why are we supposed to be so excited?"

Tim laughed and finished pulling off his socks. "Beats me," he finally replied, as he started on his pants. "Maybe it's got something to do with carrying on the family line, you know, things like that. All I can tell you is that every client I've ever seen, in and out of my own practice, has reacted in just that way."

"But why?" I persisted. "Family lines are for royalty and Rockefellers who have titles and fortunes to leave. Why should every John and Mary Doe go off into orbit because the next generation is on the way?"

14

By now, Tim was stretched out in bed. "Honey," he said, his words half-swallowed in a big yawn, "don't fight it. Let's go to sleep. It's been a really hard day and I'm beat. I've got to be in court first thing in the morning."

"I'm not fighting anything," I answered indignantly, as I climbed in beside him—and I wasn't then. "I'm just trying to get things sorted out in my mind. Good night."

The sorting out, obviously, was over for that session, but the questions arose again and again. Did grandparental elation stem from a generalized kind of hidden fear that many people have that they might not live long enough to see their own children fully grown? Is all the hoopla a way of saying, "See? I made it!"

Or is it a variation on the old theme that silently plagues all parents and makes them over-rejoice at each ordinary, successive step along the way from infancy on through breastfeeding, weaning, walking, talking, toilet training and college? Namely, that one begins as a mother and father with a wiggling, speechless, incomprehensible piece of humanity, which has as much in common with puppies and all kinds of wild animal life as it has with human beings; that walking, talking and other signs of normal growth, therefore, are heralded by the parents as wonders to behold. Because, deep down, (and they would never confess it), perhaps even in their subconscious minds, there is a nagging fear and a secret disbelief that the precious, nondescript lump of baby will ever really assume the characteristics of a man or a woman. And this, mind you, despite all the evidence in the world around!

"Maybe it's just that everyone loves a baby," Tim suggested after one of my recurrent analyses for his benefit. "You know how it is," he smiled teasingly. "Or can't you remember that far back, Grandma?"

We were at dinner in our favorite Chinese restaurant this time, and we were both feeling relaxed and good. "I remember," I laughed back. "Only seriously, darling, I'm not talking about babies. Sure, anybody in his right mind loves a baby. They're cute, they're cuddly, and each one is a miracle in its own right. I'm talking about grandparenthood. Why all the ballyhoo for that?"

"I haven't the least idea," he answered, gulping down a mouthful of Won Ton soup, "unless there are really some fringe benefits to the deal which we've so far missed. That's a possibility."

"Like what?" I challenged. Debbie had produced Melinda almost a year ago by then, and we had yet to understand why all of our friends were still reacting as if we had won First Prize in the lottery.

"How do I know?" Then Tim had his great inspiration. "I've got it," he announced. "Why don't you research it, like you do with a medical problem I ask you to run down? How's that for an approach? Why not be scientific about it?"

Why not? Tim specialized in medical jurisprudence and I sometimes helped out.

Obviously, the Academy of Medicine would not be my take-off point now, but in this era of excessive literary productivity, where printed books and booklets spring from the nation's presses like dandelions on an open lawn, there surely must be some treatise available on grandparenthood, too. Not that I planned to investigate the problem as if I were tracking source material for a Ph.D. thesis. But how could I possibly escape it, if even just through casual encounters with what modern literature usually encompasses? Why should my initiation into grandparenthood be that much different from the inundation I remembered from my original foray into motherhood?

Ah, the new mother!

Nothing, it seemed (and it still seems), is sacred to the innumerable masterpieces dotting the literary landscape in this sphere. Advice, as prolific and often as useful as the ordinary variety of garden weed, appears everywhere: what to feed; when to feed; how to feed. Breast versus Bottle; Meat versus Vegetable; Spock versus A Good Spanking;

16

Nipples, Navels, Colic and the Subconscious Mind. Ugh.

Encouraged by these recollections, however, and fortified with the knowledge that such written copiousness in these days is by no means limited to the baby bit, I began my search for the grandparenthood equivalent. Of which there were comparatively none! Some psychological tomes, of course, did make reference to grandparents, as did some sociological ones, but the emphasis was primarily on the phenomena of aging, or ramifications associated with the Nuclear Family.

I am totally discounting, incidentally, those gift shop pamphlets entitled, "What is a Grandmother?" which are printed in saccharine instead of ink, and which make the gooiest greeting cards read like poison pen letters. A representative composite of these monstrosities—and they all sound alike—assures the world in soft pastel drawings and sentimental verse that a grandmother is:

> someone to love you
> someone to spoil you
> someone to bake goodies for you
> someone to babysit you
> et cetera, et cetera, et cetera.

"I just can't believe it," I finally reported back for Tim's benefit. "I saw somewhere recently that about 30,000 books come out each year—not to mention magazine articles. And it certainly seems as if this whole country is busy with everybody telling everybody else about any and everything. Why not about grandparents?"

"Honey," Tim sounded genuinely surprised, "are you sure? I thought I saw something in the card store the other day."

"Pretty much so," I replied. "Except for Hallmark. And that stuff is pure drivel as far as I'm concerned. Do you want to do macrame, build a swimming pool, adopt a child, improve your sex life, live to ninety? Name it and I can get you the kind of written directions that should be reserved for the installation of washing machines or other mechanical equipment. But grandparents—I tell you, sweetie, I've drawn a blank."

Tim was silent for a moment and then he suddenly burst out laughing. "Maybe the silence is telling you something," he said.

"What do you mean?" I asked suspiciously, looking him belligerently in the eye.

"Well," he grinned, "if grandparenthood were something special to really sound off about, people would be telling it from the rooftops. After all, honey, when a couple of kids get set to play house, did you ever hear one of them say to the other, 'I'll be the grandpa and you be the grandma?' No sir! They always choose a Mama and a Daddy. Get it?"

"Huh!" I snorted. "I get your implication all right, but I think you're missing the mark. Even if being a grandparent doesn't raise hosannahs in anyone's soul, it's still a definite state of being. I've been a grandmother for almost two years by now, and I'm convinced that not only were my adjustments and my insights hard to come by, but they are as much a part of the life cycle as any of the Seven Stages of Man (was it seven?) that Shakespeare proclaimed. So why not talk about it freely and fully?"

The question, apparently, was mostly directed at myself. In answer to which, therefore, I decided to abandon my C.I.A. approach to my investigation and go public. Carefully, of course. Tim's vulnerability as a practicing attorney in our small, suburban community invariably subordinated my valor to my discretion.

I began this phase of my grandparenthood quest by the casual introduction of the subject into conversations with friends. The general modus operandi at first was to latch on to some vaguely related thing that had just been said or, if there were no opening, to insert the topic along with a batch of small talk about household help and dress sales. Later on, naturally, I grew more direct and bold. However

18

it was accomplished, though, it was always sort of like dropping smooth, small stones into a body of still water—and the ripples were not only many, but beyond expectation.

For example, I was having lunch one day with Janet Scott, when I suddenly, in response to some mention she had made about her son, asked point-blank, "Janet, you have two half-grown grandchildren now. How do you like being a grandmother?"

Janet looked shocked.

"Why, Edwina," she floundered, looking more pained and uncomfortable than if I had challenged something as personal and fundamental as her belief in God. "Of course, I like it. It's the greatest! It's marvelous!"

Long experience since that time has taught me that this declaration is an automatic, simple reflex on the part of the indoctrinated. Even then, however, I recognized the need to delve beyond the programming.

"Why is it marvelous, Janet?" I persisted. "Has it made any real difference in your life?"

She looked even more shocked. Then she rallied.

"For heaven's sake, Edwina," she sputtered. "They're beautiful children. I love Lisa and Johnny. Isn't that enough?"

"Is it?" I countered. "Are they even really part of your life—yours and Stewart's?"

This time I hit a home run—and I almost felt sorry. Janet's face saddened, and her voice took on a quavery sound it had not had before.

"Well, it's always bothered me—to tell the truth. Gregg and his wife live an hour away, and somehow we never have been able to get to see him and his family as much as we'd like. I remember when Johnny was really small—he's the older of the two—we'd have to get introduced all over again each time we came to visit. One time, Gregg kept rehearsing Johnny over and over again, pointing out that I was Grandma and that Stew was Pappy—they call him that.

19

Before we left, a couple of hours afterward, Gregg took Johnny over to me and asked him who I was. The poor child said 'Pappy.' Can you imagine that!"

"I sure can," I answered through a burst of laughter. "I'm going through that with Melinda right now."

Janet smiled appreciatively. "I guess it's funny in a way. Except that it's symptomatic of the relationship between grandparents and grandchildren nowadays. We're more visitors than we are members of the family."

I found this theme to be a recurrent one among most grandparents with whom I talked. It was rarely something admitted initially, of course, but it was usually a concession that was reluctantly and unhappily made once lip service had been paid to the superficialities. Evn grandparents who lived practically on top of their grandchildren often made the same complaint.

"Don't you see why?" Hilda Davis asked me during one of our frequent telephone discussions. Hilda and I were old college friends, and with her there was no need to connive or contrive. She was ten years ahead of me on the grandparent line and I respected her judgment—especially after she had agreed to let down her hair. "It's this way," she explained. "Our children basically don't want us to get too involved with their children. I guess they feel it cramps their style, or something. We, in turn, have been taught never to say too much because we're never, never supposed to interfere with our children in any way. So what does it add up to? Near or far, grandparents can only perform like empty-headed ninnies: dedicated as a Moonie disciple, dependable as the Postal Service used to be, and uncritical and mum as the Sphinx. But partners in the enterprise? Never!"

A piece here and a piece there, and gradually all the pieces of the grandparenthood puzzle began to fall into proper perspective. It was clearly apparent that something in Denmark was not all it was cracked up to be—but what exactly was it? Furthermore, could I analyze it fairly and spread the word? Also, should I?

It was the "should" that was most troubling.

"Don't do it," Tim counselled, when I announced my leanings in the direction of this book. "Why stick your neck out and get it chopped off?"

"How so?" I asked.

"Oh, you know," he said. "If you prick the grandparenthood bubble for people, they'll have a fit. They'll never admit the truth anyway, because most of them secretly believe every other grandparent is in seventh heaven, and that the reason they're not is that there's something the matter with them. They'll say you don't know what you're talking about. They'll say that just because you've soured on grandparenthood doesn't change a thing."

"But I'm not soured on grandparenthood," I protested. "You know that, darling. It's got plusses and minuses and I only want to set the record straight."

"And I only want to keep you from getting hurt." Tim put his arms around me and held me close. "Honey, a controversial subject arouses loud repercussions. Why don't you do another biography or anything innocuous? Why not play it safe?"

Tim's logic was incontrovertible, but evidently not enough to stem the tide that I had already emotionally and mentally set in motion for myself. In the end, it was a dinner party at our own home that broke the dam I was trying so hard to erect around the whole idea.

We had had a pleasant evening with lots of laughter and talk along the way, but with the subject of grandparenthood somehow rearing its head incredibly again and again. For instance, even before we sat down to eat, Ginny Howell assured me and everyone that she and Dick had had a real hassle just to come out that night.

"You know how it is," she complained loudly. "My daughter and her husband didn't see why we wouldn't babysit for their youngsters. They couldn't understand how our dinner date could be as important as theirs. I tell

21

you—I sometimes believe they think it's a *privilege* to be allowed to babysit. Maybe," she laughed, "they think we've never been close to a child before!"

Obviously, these remarks evoked many related and as many unrelated ones, but I held my peace. Nor was there very much that I permitted myself to say later on when Mary Shook confided to me that with her daughter living in California, she felt that she was being "cheated" out of her place in her grandson's life.

"It must be so wonderful to have your grandchildren nearby," she told me wistfully. "I don't even feel that I'm a grandmother most of the time. I must be missing so much."

Her sadness disturbed me, but my self-imposed silence disturbed me even more. So much so, that by midnight when we were only three couples left, I could no longer keep still.

"How do you all feel about being grandparents?" I asked suddenly, during a conversational lull. "Is it a big thing in your lives?"

There was Harry Richards and his wife, Gwen; Fred Shultz and his wife, Christine; and Tim and I. Harry was a surgeon, Gwen was a nurse, Fred was a lawyer and Christine taught psychology in a nearby university. All of us were grandparents.

The initial reaction was astonishment mixed with amusement.

"Who thinks about that?" Harry spoke up first. "It's just another life process, like going gray or losing your teeth."

Fred was more serious in his response.

"What are you really getting at, Edwina?" he asked—somewhat warily, I thought.

"Just your unexpurgated thinking," Tim answered for me. We were seated together on the sofa, facing the fireplace. The flames had settled down to a contented purr, and I leaned lazily against Tim for moral as well as physical support. "The fact is, Edwina thinks being a grandparent in this day and age is a new kind of ballgame that gets shoved under the rug the way sex used to be. She wants to drag it out and examine it—honestly and in detail. In print."

"Well, there's your starter." Fred's lawyer-urge to verbalize could always be counted on to get things moving. "Maybe the problem is just that when people think of grandparents, they think of what used to be. They don't realize or care to admit that it no longer is."

"That's true," Gwen exclaimed. "Grandma lived with us, after Grandpa died, for many years—and she was always there to turn to when you needed some talk or help. Momma was always too busy with all the other children and the chores on the farm. But Grandma, although she pitched right in on everything, always seemed to be available, no matter what. It was almost like having two mothers."

"My God!" Fred exploded with mock horror. "You mean Grandma Walton isn't just the product of T.V.'s poetic license?"

When we stopped laughing, Christine affirmed what Gwen had said. "My grandmother didn't ever live with us," she remembered nostalgically, "but we saw a lot of her and adored her. We were taught early on that she was to be respected and obeyed. My mother would have punished us severely if we ever were rude to her in any way, and we would never have dared to try it."

Fred had obviously appointed himself moderator of the unofficial forum. "OK," he now decreed. "Does anyone here fit the old-time grandparent concept that has just been introduced into evidence?"

"Are you kidding?"

"You must be crazy!"

"Good grief!"

The comments around the room were spontaneous and unanimous. Tim elaborated for everyone. "None of us are in that mold," he summarized. "The gals here don't look like grandmothers. . ."

"And aren't supposed to!" I interrupted.

"That's right," he agreed. "We all live in a youth-

23

oriented culture and growing old—or letting it show any more than you can help—is forbidden. We're all supposed to have our own lives; and that's to make sure we don't horn in on our children's. We keep busy as much as we can. We work, we travel, we play golf—all of it occupational therapy to prevent us from being meddling, full-time, old-time grandparents."

There was a bitter note in Tim's remarks that surprised me. Before I could say anything, though, another verbal deluge flooded the place.

"It's strictly hands-off-deal," Harry exploded, "unless they need some money. You can always bail them out. That's the one exception."

"Not just money!" Gwen's vehemence matched her husband's. "Whenever they get into trouble, Mother and Daddy are supposed to stand by and help. In sickness, you must be available for moral support, at least, and financial assistance, as need be—but whatever the problem, their needs take priority over yours. When things are going well, you're lucky if you get an occasional call."

"The root problem," Christine injected her commentary in her psychologist role, "is that our children are incredibly insecure. The older generation represents a threat to them in their personal struggles to prove themselves. They only want applause from their parents, and categorize all other comment or advice as negative criticism. Grandchildren become pawns in this competitive game—and family relationships suffer."

At this stage, Fred intervened. "Hey, hold on, all of you," he ordered, like an irate judge taking control of a turbulent courtroom. "Calm down."

The suddenness of the command brought us to an abrupt halt. Then we looked at Fred's exaggeratedly solemn face and burst out laughing. The tension that had become almost as visible and disturbing as a low-hanging mountain fog began to lift.

"Now listen," Fred said, grabbing the chairmanship

24

reigns again. "Don't you realize what we've been saying? Yes, grandparents aren't what they used to be, but if they've changed, it's their children who are responsible for the change. And if you ask me, Edwina, that's your focal point. Grandparenthood is only what children want it to be—what they let it become. If you're really serious about the whole idea, check this aspect out. I'd bet my eyeteeth that the clues are hidden in your own parenthood."

They all got up to go almost immediately after this dissertation of Fred's. I sensed a kind of overall embarrassment—the way interviewees often react when they have spouted forth and then been told that they've been on Candid Camera. Harry triggered the Exodus by remembering he had early rounds the next morning and in just a few minutes more, the group had gone.

Fred's words in particular, however, and the talk in general would not leave my mind as Tim and I almost automatically busied ourselves emptying ashtrays and cleaning up. Usually, these chores after a party were a fun session, highlighted by a gay rehash of who had said what and when. This time, I was obviously preoccupied and unresponsive to any attempts at humor.

"Honey," Tim finally insisted upon my undivided attention. "What's bothering you? You've been plumping up that same sofa pillow five different times."

"Oh." I put the pillow down. "I don't know how to put it, sweetie. It's just that they all sounded so unhappy when they were going on about their grandparent role. I never heard them come across like that before. Even *you!*" I finished accusingly.

For an answer, Tim pulled me down beside him on the sofa I had just neatened. "Let it wait," he insisted when I started to protest. "Let's talk this out once and for all. Now—why should it surprise you that I, too, am very much aware that modern grandparenthood leaves a lot to be desired? Don't forget, all of us have been subjected to the traditional grandparent ballyhoo for years and years. And even when

25

we should know better, the reality can be a disturbing let-down. Did you think that just because you're more vocal that I'm oblivious?"

"No." I looked at Tim carefully. "But you never say anything. You just let me go on and on."

"Do I have much chance?" he asked teasingly. "But if you want me to spell it out, I will. Yes. I don't know exactly what I thought being a grandfather would be like, but I guess way down, deep inside, I had been harboring the usual delusions. And yes—in many ways the whole thing has been a definite let-down."

As Tim spoke, it was as if his declaration were the sign from heaven for which I had been secretly waiting—as clear a call to action as reveille in an army camp. And just like that, the hesitation and the indecision in which I had been wallowing for so long took shape and jelled into purpose that was near concrete. Suddenly, I could see it all, and it was beautifully clear.

Many grandparents—especially after the birth of their first grandchild—go through a kind of post-partum depression. Legend has led them to expect themselves to be "raptured" immediately on to cloud number nine. Reality reveals that this isn't so; and the feelings of guilt and incompetence that so often accompany this realization—the burdensome misconception that no other "normal" grandparents are similarly afflicted—can convert the whole grandparenthood experience into a chapter from the Book of Job.

So? There was nothing for me to do but tell it as it is. I would spell out the highs and the lows. I would foster realistic expectations and spread the word that there are no longer rights, privileges and immunities automatically conferred upon the Holy Order of Grandparents. I would remind everyone who bothered to listen that grandparents are people—that they were people before they became grandparents, and that they will go on being people afterwards; that because they are people, they need never apologize for their individual adjustments to their grandparenthood any more than they would for the singularity of their fingerprints. I would assure one and all that there is no miraculous transformation that takes place—like the water into wine—when a grandchild is born.

Maybe Tim was right. Maybe I was girding up to fight City Hall. Maybe few grandparents would pay any attention to my words. Maybe others would even resent them—but the truth would have to be its own excuse for being.

Besides, you could never tell. Many a lone voice, crying in the wilderness before, started a chorus that echoed round the world.

Chapter II

ROOTS

THERE are three basic, controlling facts which should—but obviously don't—govern grandparental expectations. They are: that grandparenthood is the normal by-product of parenthood; that the one stems literally from the other; and that it is a natural law of the universe that water never rises higher than its source.

Unfortunately, any rational consideration of these premises is hindered by the further fact that by the time one gets to be a grandparent, there is a definite tendency to misremember or entirely forget all that was endured getting there. And as usual, it was Tim who made me acutely aware of this grandparental myopia when I first announced at breakfast the day after the party, that I was going to do this book, and that my starting point would be a backward look into my experiences as a mother—just as Fred had indicated.

"O.K.," Tim began, somewhat reluctantly. "I guess if you must, you must."

"I must," I assured him promptly.

"Then that's that," he responded unenthusiastically, but without any further resistance. "Just do it as if you were under oath. And if you need any help jogging your memory, check things out with me. For instance, do you recall your first reaction to Debbie after she was born?"

I hesitated. "Why, I'm sure I was excited and pleased and proud. Wasn't I?" I finished lamely.

"You howled," Tim informed me. "The first time I came to see you, you were sobbing because Debbie had just been carried in to your room a little while before, and her eyes crossed and she kept sneezing and there was vomitous dripping out the side of her loosely-held mouth. I couldn't convince you that all babies do this kind of thing, and that she'd straighten out in time."

"You're right!" I exclaimed, as it all came back to me. "I thought she was ugly and we'd never get her married off. Even worse, I thought I was a terrible unnatural mother because everything I'd ever read had led me to believe that one look at my newborn should have enslaved me for life—the way a single spark can start a fire that can burn down a whole house. Instead, I took that look and was horrified."

Tim laughed. "Pure mythology," he said. "Maybe so for some, but not so for many."

"But mythology is exactly what I've been resenting so in the grandparent role," I realized suddenly. "I've clean forgotten that it drove me wild in the parental sphere, too."

And it had. Even when I was expecting Debbie, I could not bear the constant disparities I encountered everywhere between Motherhood fiction and fact. Despite the *Ladies Home Journal* and Margaret Mead, pregnancy in my eyes had never had a "spiritual, glowing" look nor could it offer mute testimony of any meaningful significance. When I stared into my mirror during that period, my face seemed flatter than last week's soufflé and (too often) more set and agonized than rigor mortis on the second day. When I walked on the street, I appeared to be going and coming at the same time: waddling like a penguin and balancing carefully like a tightrope walker on stilts without a safety net. Some beauty to behold!

Tim and I sat at the table for nearly an hour longer, dragging out and reliving some of the ridiculous, deeply-rooted fantasies that had plagued our early parenthood. After three more cups of coffee and much laughter, I made an important observation.

"Remembering all the gobbledygook that surrounded parenthood," I said, "is incredibly consoling. It makes it just a little more tolerable that the world is also filled with tall tales about grandparenthood. I tell you, sweetie, my hat's off to Fred. The clues to understanding what being a grandparent *is* do lie in understanding what being a parent *was*. Also in what the relationship between the parents and the children were. . ."

"And are." Tim stood up and stretched. "You can take it from there, honey. I'm on my way."

For weeks and weeks afterwards, I was busy taking it from there. I kept trying to find some correlation between Debbie and us and then, Debbie and Melinda and us. It was not easily apparent. Especially since I was searching out our parental roots with Tim's warnings about my entire grandparental project echoing ominously and discouragingly in my ears.

At first, in my backward glances, I would only think that in Debbie's growing up, there had been very little of the spectacular. She was of good intelligence, had always done well in school and had behaved within acceptable bounds of propriety. At least, as far as I knew.

When she was very small, my maternal *raison d'etre* had been to avoid spoiling her—and never was any revolution for independence more bravely waged. "Having a baby," I had proclaimed, "is like having another person come to live with us. We can all live happily together only if the baby is trained to fit in right from the start. Otherwise, we will wind up with an unreasoning, monstrous tyrant, instead of a companionable child."

I had been adamant on this count, and fortunately, so had Tim. We both abhorred the kind of dedication that was the vogue in Debbie's babyhood: Get up at night and make sure your baby is breathing. Smile at him and speak

31

sweetly when he wakes you three or four times, or you might hurt his feelings. Pick him up when he cries, because it's cruel to let him scream. Find out why. He can't tell you, but try a drink, a toy, or just a funny face. Feed him on demand; change him. Feed him again and change him again. Even though your head is aching, "laugh, clown, laugh" and bring the bottle; even though your back is breaking, get a clean diaper.

Our vigilante approach in this area apparently succeeded. As Debbie grew, a reasonable facsimile of the kind of person we had hoped she would become began to appear. She was polite, cooperative and generally someone we could acknowledge freely, without wincing. If we had bordered occasionally on the fringe of benevolent despotism during her childhood—and we may have—she seemed unaware of it; if we had erred constantly in our efforts to make her home life an experimental slice of the outside world rather than a Sunday School version of the Garden of Eden minus, of course, the snake, she never complained.

"Until adolescence," Tim reminded me promptly, when I had come this far in my saga. "Suddenly, everything we said was wrong and everything we did was a great source of embarrassment to her. Remember?"

Would I ever forget?

I could lecture competently and profitably to every Woman's Club in a radius of one hundred miles, but if I said "Hello, Susie, I saw your mother today" to Susie, who was one of Debbie's visiting classmates, I could count on Debbie's horrified, "Mother! How could you?" afterwards.

"Good Lord," I told Tim, shuddering, even after many years, at the recollection. "She used to make me feel like a backward Mongolian idiot! Remember the day she told me she hated me when I wouldn't let her go to a party—it was in high school—because we knew the kids were bringing in liquor?"

"It was hard for us," he answered gently, "but it was hard for her, too. She had become aware of the peer pressures around her and she didn't know how to cope."

For a moment I was silent. It is amazing how hindsight can give you twenty/twenty vision. Looking back, I could suddenly see the overall problem that had dominated that period. "Peer pressures were strictly *social* pressures," I analyzed it aloud for Tim's benefit. "What did the girls all want? They wanted to be popular. That was the password. Popular with the other girls and/or at least with one boy. Grades didn't matter. Being asked to parties, to football games, to dances—that was important."

"That's right," Tim agreed, "and in college, it became the hunt to find a husband. Miserable business."

I had to smile at Tim's earnestness. As the father of a daughter, Tim had long ago become an ardent feminist. His enlarged understanding of the inequities that exist between the sexes would have made Gloria Steinem's version seem mid-Victorian.

"In fact, maybe it was always the hunt to find a husband," he said, after a brief pause. "Maybe that's really what's behind the high school business, too. You know, honey, if I had any say in it, I'd segregate one boy off for every girl, way back in kindergarten. Then the kids would be free to study, to play, to develop their talents without having to worry if they'd ever find someone to marry, and having it hound them all along the way."

I knew even better than Tim exactly what he was talking about. Granted that there are some girls who are born beautiful and bright, and who walk through life from infancy onward with a convoy of ardent admirers. Most of us, unfortunately, don't have the sex appeal of a Farrah Fawcett Majors or the self-confidence and charm of a Barbara Walters. We are not homely and we are not pretty. The usual terminology to describe our physical attributes is "nice-looking" to "average"; the highest praise our personalities and social prowess merit is, "She's O.K."

Translating all of this to specifics means that most of us ordinary females have to engage in endless maneuvers to

33

find a man. Women's Lib may change the United States Constitution, but there is no force on earth that can tamper with this basic scheme of things. They may "shack up" instead of marrying, they may even just "sleep around," but the need for someone of their own, someone to love and be loved by, someone to share their lives, is as fundamental and inescapable as secondary sex characteristics. It is the essence of marriage for which they are searching, no matter by what name the rose is called.

For myself, my conscription into the front lines of the mating game started in my early teens. Included was every possible strategy to forestall social exile, from going stag to open dances (sheer horror!) and braving blind dates that were sure losers (oh, the pure agony!), to accepting escort service to school affairs from a succession of "weirdos" who seemed—not merely in retrospect, but even then—as non-human as creatures described emerging from flying saucers. To this day, I cannot bear the sound of certain old tunes like "June in January" because they transport me immediately onto the prom floor, up against the smelly, sweating and heavy-breathing body of an awkward young man with whom the only thing I had in common was the exact spot we both somehow found each time I moved my foot.

Debbie, alas, was obviously no more a Playboy Bunny than I had been. Her ordeal began with dancing class along about the seventh grade, when the measure of an evening's success was the number of times a girl was asked to dance and by how many. If I could have bribed or beaten some of those characters to ensure that Debbie was on the floor even half the time, I would have. But when I merely vaguely hinted in this direction, Debbie reacted as if I had threatened her with an axe.

"Mother!" she screamed. "You can't! Oh, I'd die if you ever even tried something like that. I'd die, I really would! I'd never go to school again!"

"Now, sweetie," I hurriedly retreated, "don't get so

upset. Of course, I wouldn't do anything drastic. I was just thinking out loud."

Thereafter, of course, I reserved all my thinking out loud for Tim. Every Tuesday night, after Debbie returned in defeat from the next session ("Oh, Mother, I only got asked twice—and both times it was the class goon!") and we had tried to comfort her and then sent her to bed, Tim and I would hold a secret conference of our own. Extremely secret, you understand, because Debbie would only have been demoralized or shocked by our conversations. We whispered furtively in our bedroom with more caution apparently than the Watergaters laid their plans; and one time, I distinctly remember that we decided to talk in our parked car in the driveway for absolute privacy until, after a half-hour, the local police officer flashed his light in our startled faces and asked Tim suspiciously, "Is there anything wrong, Counsellor?"

"I can't bear to see her so unhappy," I told Tim one night, after we had just finished going through another round of the dancing class with Debbie. "She won't drop out because that would amount to an open admission that she couldn't make it. But I don't know what to do."

"What's the matter with those idiots?" Tim raged, as frustrated as I. "Nobody's asking them to marry her or even date her. Why can't they just dance with her a couple of times? She's as nice looking as most of those kids in her class, and a lot smarter than almost any."

"Oh, Tim," I wailed back. "It's such a dismal thing and I remember it so well. Sitting on the sidelines, trying to look bright and excited and shrivelling up inside with embarrassment because everyone else can see that no one has picked you for a partner. Only it's much, much worse for me to go through it with Debbie."

It is a fact of life that having a child is a means of extending one's protoplasm outward, thus exposing oneself doubly to pleasure and pain. Perhaps the passage of time had healed the edge of my own experiences or perhaps it was just motherhood—or both. Whatever it was, I ached terribly for Debbie but could do little about it.

Oh, I tried. In one of our meetings, I came up with one proposal after another which Tim voted down so rapidly that my mind began to feel as full of holes as the target board on a rifle range. No. We could not ask Margie Lewis to make Junior go waltzing next week with Debbie. What if it got out? And knowing Junior, it would! No. We could not tackle the dancing school teacher and arrange for some kind of merciful intercession. It would soon be quite obvious—and wouldn't that be worse? No. No. No. Tim would not join me in being parent-chaperones. Would dancing with her *father* improve anything?

Finally, Tim asked: "What about the other mothers? What do they do? Surely Debbie isn't the only wallflower?"

"I honestly don't know," I answered. "They don't talk about it. The way they tell it, their children are 'having a ball.' *Aren't they sweet? Isn't it just wonderful for them to get together like this?* You'd think social unpopularity were something like B.O. or halitosis—never to be mentioned in public. The only one who has ever been open about it is Gertie Smith. You know, Gertie: she'll talk about anything, from her bowel habits to her mother-in-law's sex life. Well, she's just furious about what Amy is going through and is going to pull her out—says she's not going to let her daughter wait around for takers—like the old time slaves on the auction block. But Debbie insists on sticking it out."

Eventually, of course, dancing class ended. I soon realized, however, that they were but preliminary skirmishes before the big war that loomed ahead. In the high school years particularly, every social event on the calendar erupted in our family circle like a Pearl Harbor attack on our domestic tranquility.

"There's a Christmas dance in two weeks," Debbie would report mournfully. "I wish I could go."

"Now, sweetie," I would reply as cheerfully as I could, "maybe someone will ask you. There's still time."

"Nope. They're all lined up already." Debbie would

permit no phony optimism. "I guess boys just don't like me. I can't giggle and act smart like lots of the girls. I never know what to say."

In the spring of Debbie's freshman year, I had my first major inspiration. It was the result of a consultation with my friend, Hilda. We talked frequently on the telephone, although we rarely had time to actually meet in person, since Hilda lived about an hour's distance from our town. We had gone through some of what Debbie was enduring during our college days together, and I turned often to her disembodied voice for moral support.

"Of course," I told her one day, "you don't have to go through this anymore because you've got two boys."

"Don't be ridic, Edwina," she replied laughingly. "O.K., so they don't have to wait to be asked, but they have adolescent trauma of their own. Acne, for one thing—you should see Jimmy!—and shyness. They want to get in on things, but they're awkward and scared to take the initiative. Besides, boys are more prone to smoking, sex experimentation, drugs—just name it! After all, you don't have to worry that some pretty, young thing is going to hang her illegitimate baby on your son, do you?"

It was at this point, apropos of nothing, and in what Tim fondly called my non sequitur brand of logic, that I conceived my first and last desperate solution to our on going crisis.

"Hilda," I said excitedly, can we borrow your Jimmy for one night for the Spring Hop?"

"Pimples and all?" Hilda chuckled delightedly.

"You won't have to do a thing," I went on eagerly. "We'll drive down and get him; we'll bring him back. Even if he can't dance much. . ."

"He can't," Hilda interrupted.

"He can just show up with Debbie and jump around the floor some. Everyone will see that Debbie made it to the dance, and maybe that will break the ice."

"Say no more," Hilda declared. "What are friends for? I

see what you mean. He'll make excellent window-dressing for Debbie. He's sixteen next month—nearly two years older than Debbie and he's almost six feet tall—when he stands up straight. Now tell me what and where and when."

Lining up Hilda was easy compared to the next job of selling Debbie and Tim on the project. Finally, reason (mine) prevailed, and on the appointed night, Debbie, all dressed up, and Tim and I embarked on the hour drive to get Jimmy.

Poor Jimmy! He was pale and nervous, and swallowed again and again over an Adam's apple that stood out on his skinny neck like a golf ball. His palms were unmistakably wet when he shook hands. It turned out that not only had he never participated in this kind of function before, but that he had obviously been drafted on this occasion against his better judgment. He became terribly carsick on the hour-long drive over to the gym, began to throw up violently the moment we arrived, and, spread on the backseat like a corpse, had to be carted back home at once.

"It's no use," Debbie sobbed, after we deposited Jimmy and started on the fourth and final hour back to our own house. "I'll never get to anything. I'll be an old maid."

"For heaven's sake, Debbie," I replied, worn out by then with a four-hour drive that could have taken us practically from Pittsburgh to Washington, D.C., "even if you don't date now, it doesn't mean you never will. I had slow going when I was your age also, but didn't I wind up with your father?"

"Sure," Tim tried to be funny. "I saved your mother from being an old maid."

"Rubbish," I swung right back. "I could have married a couple of other guys—and probably would have, if I hadn't fallen in love with you." Then I addressed Debbie again. "Honey, stop crying and listen to me. You'll have your share of fun and dates. Be patient. And you'll get married some day, too. There are lots of boys out there, and when they get the matrimonial urge, they have to marry girls—not horses. You'll see."

"Oh, Mother," Debbie was unconvinced; "you just don't understand!"

It was Tim—God Bless him—who offered the only words of comfort and encouragement on the whole Jimmy fiasco. "Dearest," he told me later on that night when we were in bed and I lay in his arms, crying over my own disappointment. "Let's not make mountains out of molehills. I know you wanted to help Debbie and you're extra hurt because it fizzled and she doesn't even appreciate why you did it. But honey, you've got to have some of the faith and expectancy you keep preaching to her. One of these days, there'll be a breakthrough and you can help her then. But she's got to do it by herself. It's her life. It's her problem."

The breakthrough, so accurately predicted by Tim-Nostradamus, took place about eight months later, when Debbie was in her sophomore year. She came home from school one day with the usual announcement of an upcoming school dance and her impossible dream of going. Only this time, there was a variation on the theme.

"Mother," she said hesitantly, pausing to take another sip of milk, "you remember that boy I told you talks to me sometimes? David Jones? Remember him?"

I nodded.

"Well," she went on, "he's not much, but he'd be someone who could take me to the dance. So how can I get him to ask me?"

How? Never having been a Cleopatra, I was not at all sure how to proceed. Finally, I said, "Why don't you bring up the subject tomorrow? Ask him if he's going and that might give him the idea."

The next day, Debbie came home from school and reported that she had carried out her orders to the letter. Result: No, he was not going to the dance.

What now?

"Well," I spoke slowly, wanting to inspire confidence in

Debbie by trying to sound like the Delphic Oracle, "since he missed the cue today, you'll have to be more direct tomorrow. Tell him you're not going either because no one has asked you yet. Then let him know that you wish you could go—if someone would only ask you. Unless he's really retarded. . ."

"Oh, he's not that bad," Debbie broke in immediately.

"Then he should respond with an offer to take you," I finished, as if it were all a *fait accompli.*

And it was!

The next day Debbie flew into the house after school and grabbed me in a great bear hug. "Mother, it worked!" she almost screamed in her excitement. "I said what you said I should and he said what you said he would—and we're going to the dance on Friday!"

Her euphoric state lasted almost the rest of the week. Debbie apparently informed everyone in and out of her class that she was going to the dance with David. Being asked, I realized, was as important as going. She insisted on a new dress so that she could brag about it the way all the others did, and we practiced some dances (I was the male lead) just to make sure.

On Friday afternoon, she came home from school with her flag clearly flying at half-mast.

"What's happened, dear?" I asked, not daring to voice terrible thought that he might have reneged.

"Oh, Mother," she said, too upset to bother with the cookies waiting on the kitchen table, "all the girls were talking about their corsages today. Did you know their dates are bringing them flowers to wear because it's a Formal? I'll be the only one there without a corsage!"

For a moment, I felt like reminding her, "But at least you'll be there and you've never been before!" Her distress, however, founded or unfounded, could not be ignored. "Debbie," I said, "maybe David will bring a corsage when he comes to call for you."

"No." She was as absolutely definite as a T.V. announcer

40

reading off yesterday's baseball scores. "All the girls said their fellows asked them the colors of their dresses so the flowers would match. That's how it's done. But David never even asked me anything. I guess he doesn't know."

"Oh." Still, I could not give up. Where Debbie was concerned, I would always refuse to abandon the ship until we were completely submerged. "Honey," I offered my next idea hopefully, "maybe David's mother will remind him about a corsage."

"Nope. She's out of town." Debbie, as usual, was adamantly negative.

"But, sweetie," I said next, "is it so important?"

"Is what so important?" Tim had just come home at this point, in time to hear my last question. "What's the matter with you two anyway? I came home early from the office to see my best girl off properly for her big night. And look at the two of you—with long, long faces. What's up?"

Debbie explained, and as she spoke, we could understand why the corsage was so important. Going to the dance was her dream come true and it had to be done with all the trappings. Did Cinderella go to the ball in a pumpkin or a coach?"

"Do you see what I mean, Daddy?" she finished wistfully. "I wanted everything to be just right. I didn't want it to be second-rate in any way. Especially my first time."

Tim saw and I saw. There was a closeness among the three of us in the kitchen. Then Tim brightened.

"I've got it!" he exclaimed. "I'll get the corsage myself. No one will know who got it and that'll be that!"

It was an inspiration.

"Just you hold on," Tim called, as he started out of the house. "Now you get yourself ready, Debbie. I'll be back in the hour." Then, turning around to me, he asked, "What kind should I get, honey?"

"Red, red roses," I answered promptly. "I love them."

Then I hurried Debbie upstairs to bathe and dress and put on her fancy clothes. We were both exhilarated again, although Debbie was still leery of something going wrong.

Suddenly, she poked her head out of the top of the slip she was putting on and said: "Mother, what if David brings a corsage and I'm wearing Daddy's? I can't go with two, can I?"

We both laughed. "Don't you worry," I improvised promptly. "We'll hide Daddy's roses in my bedroom. If David shows with a corsage, we'll pin his on you. If he's empty-handed, we'll go in the other room and get Daddy's."

"But what will David think when he sees it?" Debbie worried next. "Won't it embarrass him?"

"Of course not," I responded emphatically. "If he doesn't know enough to get his own, chances are he'll think the flowers came with your dress. And the kids at school would never even imagine that it was your father—not David—who provided them."

And that was exactly how it was. Tim returned shortly with an elaborate, white satin-ribboned, huge, red-rose corsage that could have completely hidden a size 40-D bust. We put it in the bedroom as planned, and sure enough, David arrived with a tiny cluster of sweet peas which Debbie received enthusiastically, and fastened on her left shoulder with all the pride of a war hero parading his medals. Her big, blue eyes seemed to be lit by a dozen candles and her voice shook with excitement as she kissed us and said good-by.

Tim and I stood in the front doorway and watched as she floated down the path into the car, where David's father sat waiting to do the driving honors—since David's Junior License didn't permit night driving. We stood close together in that doorway for several minutes after Mr. Jones had pulled away, each of us silently, acutely aware that another door in our parenthood had opened wide.

Even writing about that night, years after it was over, could make me smile. And it was with just such a nostalgic kind of smile on my face that I greeted Tim when he came

42

into my study the other day, to see how far I had gotten with my trek backward into our history as parents.

"Remember that night?" I asked, still smiling at the memory, and filling him in briefly on my progress.

"Forever," he replied, settling into the rocker beside my desk. "It's carved in stone on my heart. And I also remember what we did afterwards. Do you?"

"Of course."

We had had no dinner and it was late. I was in jeans and an old blue T-shirt, too exhausted with the emotional tension of the whole episode to want to change.

"So," Tim recalled, laughing as he spoke, "you stuck that monstrous corsage I had gotten for Debbie on your front. . ."

"Because we'd paid for it," I interrupted gaily, "and there was no sense letting it go to waste!"

"And we went over to Dino's Hamburger Joint for a quick bite," he went on, acknowledging my comment with a grin. "And there you sat, happy as the winner of the Kentucky Derby with the wreath around his neck, munching away on a mile-long hot dog covered with onions—while everybody in the place, including Dino, kept wanting to know what was the celebration: your birthday or our anniversary!"

We both laughed again at the recollection. Then I said, "You know, sweetie, it's funny now but it wasn't funny then, was it?"

"It was excruciating," he amplified. "We used to get into knots over Debbie's growing up. We sure went through a lot—the illnesses along the way, the disciplinary problems, the emotional hassles. Sometimes, I didn't think we'd make it."

"But we did," I answered promptly, "and that's what counts. Besides, isn't that what being a parent is all about—even if it turns you prematurely gray?"

"I guess so," he admitted reluctantly. Then he added, almost with surprise: "But it was worth it, too. I wouldn't have missed it for the world. After all, you grow old anyway."

"Nor I." As I thoughtfully agreed, it was as if a sudden light went on in the murky shadows of my mind. "Honey," I exclaimed, "that's the basic clue! If being a parent is hard, why should anyone expect being a grandparent to be any better or a cinch? Grandparenthood is merely an extension of parenthood; not a new state of being, but a continuation of the old. Different! Yes. New frustrations, new hopes, new hurts—yet still the same old song; just the second verse."

"But worth it," Tim reminded me, and again I agreed.

It was only a starter, of course, sort of a panoramic glimpse at the overall phenomenon of grandparenthood. Somehow, though, it was all the rope I needed to stop worrying about the torpedoes and move full steam ahead.

Chapter III

ON THE ROAD TO MANDALAY

THE development of a fully certified grandparent from a parent is a slow evolutionary process. It encompasses many of the Darwinian concepts—particularly survival of the fittest—but it is highlighted by one major difference. Instead of the usual gradual merging, the metamorphosis into grandparenthood is characterized by a definite, sharp and recognizable point at which the final stage begins: Specifically (and hopefully), the marriage of one's offspring.

Yes. It happened. Debbie got married. As Tim used to say jokingly but accurately whenever her spirits needed a lift: statistically, at least, the odds were always in her favor.

We even have the traditional wedding album to prove it. There are pictures of every gasp of the momentous occasion: Debbie putting on her veil; Debbie being escorted to the car by Tim; Debbie moving down the aisle, et cetera. My own favorite is one showing the three of us standing together on the back patio. The huge old walnut trees can be seen in the distance; the overhanging sky is a clear blue with bits of white fluff; the bride, flanked by her mother and father, is a vision of shining joy—and there is absolutely nothing in any of the faces to indicate the hell and high water we had all been through in arriving at that historic moment.

Obviously, one dance with David Jones did not produce the kind of dramatic transformation in Debbie's social life that was accomplished for the Sleeping Beauty by the appropriate prince. It was a start, of course, and for that Tim and I were properly grateful, although Debbie complained all the way to her high school graduation. There were high times and low times and it eventually reached the point where Tim's greeting each evening on his return home echoed the words of that famous news commentator who used to begin each broadcast with, "And what kind of a day has this been?" My response, accordingly, used to make me sound as if I were reporting fluctuations in the daily stock market prices.

By the age of seventeen, however, when she was ready to leave for college, Debbie had developed enough of a conversational "line" and breasts to give her the necessary, although still minimal, self-confidence to face higher educational life—which included, incidentally, the pursuit of a Bachelor of Science degree in nursing. We were no longer privy to the blow-by-blow accounts of her successes and failures, but the feeling of reprieve that Tim and I briefly and blissfully experienced soon gave way to new concerns.

In the first place, there was a whole new adjustment that Tim and I had to make to Debbie's departure. We had been so busy worrying about her adjustment to college that we had never even realized that we would have one of our own.

"It's incredible how I miss that girl," I told Tim almost tearfully one night when we were sitting down to dinner all alone. "I keep expecting her to come dashing in all the time. Sometimes, I look at the clock and find myself wondering why she hasn't gotten home from school yet. It's crazy."

"No, it isn't," Tim answered, trying to keep it light. "You know, they say that an amputee keeps feeling pain in his leg after it's been cut off. So why shouldn't you miss her?"

I wasn't consoled. "Do you think she misses us?" I asked next, after a brief interval during which Tim said a quick grace.

"Nope," Tim was annoyingly definite. Honey," he said, "have you forgotten what we always used to say? That a father and mother are like two people who've answered an ad which reads: 'Wanted: young, strong couple, willing to work all day and all night, if necessary. No time off, no pay—just satisfaction.' Didn't you always insist that filial devotion comes only with maturity? That until it comes, evidences of affection from children spring not from love but more from their need for and appreciation of the security parents represent—with a little loyalty thrown in?"

"I know." There was no arguing with Tim's philosophy, but I still felt sad.

It is perhaps the most difficult lesson of parenthood to realize that the whole thing is like a one-sided love affair. And some never do. Although our children are the stuff from which our very lives are made, we are but a diminishing part of theirs. The weaning of the young only starts in infancy. The process actually is never-ending—and the parting that comes with college is but another station on the way to the cross.

"Darling," Tim tried again to cheer me up, "why don't you start doing some of the things you've always wanted to do now that you're freer? Take a course or learn to sew. . ."

"Good Lord," I interrupted, "are you serious? I know Debbie's not here and I have more time, but I also am constantly aware that things are going on. Why, I'd feel as if I were fiddling while Rome was burning! Which reminds me," I added worriedly, checking my wrist, "I thought we'd give her a ring tonight. See how she's getting on."

Giving "Debbie a ring tonight" incidentally, was another problem area in our new way of Debbie's college life. Alexander Graham Bell may truly have marvelled at what God through him had wrought, but I'm sure he never envisioned the great temptation and economic burden the telephone would become to every lonely parent with a child away from home.

"Edwina," Tim would explode every month with the arrival of our usual, unusual telephone bill, "are you trying to break the bank? Just look at this! Some families don't pay so much in rent!"

What could I say? Nowhere in all the lovely literature that colleges put out do they even mention that telephone costs are as inherent an expense of higher education as tuition. We, as novice payers, might have been expected to overlook this hefty "extra," but surely someone in Admissions must realize what goes on. Or are all of them so far removed from parenthood that they really believe we leave our young in the academic forest to fend for themselves for the first time—and never even call up to see what's happened?

As significant as the disastrous economics of telephoning, moreover, is its even more crucial aspect as a symbol of parental surveillance. Oh, it's fine for a college young man or woman to phone home if they so choose, but the reverse is definitely less acceptable. Inequitable, you say? But isn't it all?

"This is her bid for independence," Tim cautioned me as we drove away from the campus that first day. "We'll keep in touch, of course, but mostly, let it be hands-off."

Some independence! I thought, as I sat back wearily and grunted for a reply. We had outfitted her with a wardrobe that was on the trousseau level; we were paying for her keep; we were available for whatever help she needed; if she got into trouble—heaven forbid—we were legally, liable and emotionally vulnerable and morally responsible.

The whole issue, fortunately, was purely theoretical at first. Debbie, in the beginning, before she found her niche in the campus jungle, kept calling us for reassurance and occasional advice, and obviously, we were always responsive. Expensive? Breathes there a parent with soul so dead that he would ever refuse to accept charges for a child's collect call?

Eventually, of course, Debbie made a satisfactory adjustment to her roommate, her classes, her growing social life, and the telephoning became more infrequent and sporadic. I, in turn, was left dangling at the other end of the silent telephone, wrestling with the temptation just "to give her a ring" and see how she was doing. Night after night, I would look at the ugly, black instrument the way Eve must have looked at the snake; and too often, like Eve, I succumbed.

"She'll think you're interfering," Tim would remind me warningly.

"But the whole thing's unfair," I would grumble back. "Am I supposed to stop caring about what happens to her just because she's away from home?"

It was unfair, but as I was beginning to find out, the whole parenthood deal was unfair, too. Certainly, the ordinary tribulations of advanced parent life read like a chapter from the Book of Job: To be gentle but firm, liberal but never unprincipled, directive but never controlling, critical but never discouraging, concerned but never inquisitive, helpful but never, never interfering. In many ways, it's like trying to walk a high wire in Madison Square Garden without a safety net, when you've never even been trained to manage a balance beam on the ground. Who can do it? In the end, anyway, grown sons and daughters view their successes as evidence of their own great abilities; the failures are inevitably attributed to something you did or else, should have done, in raising them. There is—with few exceptions—no winning, and the only consolation in the whole scheme lies in the exquisite poetic justice of the fact that someday our children will be parents also.

Actually, neither Tim nor I ever did resolve the To-Call-Debbie-or-Not-To-Call-Debbie issue, which remained a continual, good-humored tug-of-war between us, with the scorecard reading like a never-ending championship bout

49

("Both fighters are in the center of the ring exchanging hard body blows to the mid-section!"), with no final decision. Fortunately—on this count, at least—it became a very secondary concern in our mutual college career as we entered the next phase of Debbie's higher education: Men.

Because now, unlike the high school struggle for social survival, the stakes were higher. No longer was Debbie aiming at casual conquests on an ego-building level; no longer were we witnessing the rookie maneuvers of a mock battle. Her avowed goal was Love and Marriage and she was playing for keeps. Had she even tithed one-tenth of her energy and determination in this regard to her studies, she would have made Phi Beta Kappa for sure and Tim and I would have been spared the constant, private fear that we shared throughout those four years that she wouldn't make it. As is, that she and her like-minded friends did pass has always been a minor miracle or a major scandal to Tim and me—depending on our alternating moods.

Debbie's rationale, apparently, was to latch on to one likely prospect after another, look it over carefully to see if it met the legal size requirements and then—as any conscientious fisherman would—throw it back in if it were unsuitable. The trouble was that in the interval between the catch and the discarding, Tim and I would hold our breath waiting for her final decision while we looked with horror at some of the specimens she brought home.

"Do you realize," Tim would whisper to me when we would hide out in our bedroom on a sampling week-end to console each other, "that that *thing* in there with Debbie is being considered by her as a possible husband?"

"Oh, Tim," I would whisper back, "can you just imagine *that* as a son-in-law?"

Those being pre-grandparenthood days, I never even went the extra mile to realize that a son-in-law would also be the father of our grandchildren. Which was probably all to the good, anyway. It was agony enough to live through a procession of gruesome candidates—some of whom should have been interspersed in a police line-up—and maintain a calm exterior throughout their overnight stay.

There was a Larry, for instance. Debbie's prepublication publicity had led us to expect a Tarzan with the mind of an Einstein. After meeting him, we could understand where she had picked up this misconception since it was immediately apparent that that was exactly the way he thought of himself. His arrogance and self-esteem were incredible. He marched into our nice, suburban, middle-class home the way Nero would have picked his way into his slave's quarters; and he ordered me around in the same fashion.

His first words were, "How do you do? It's been a long drive. I'd like a hot cup of coffee."

His next full command, directed at me with a condescending recognition of my housekeeping role, was, "I'm somewhat tired. If you get my suitcase, I'd like to be shown to my room and lie down for a nap. Would you lead the way?"

When we got to the guest room (he never offered to carry the bag) he stretched out on the bed on top of my best spread and said through a yawn, "It's a little chilly in here. Do you have a blanket?"

Speechless with fury by this time, I walked to the closet in silence, pulled a blanket off the shelf, went over to the bed and held it out. Instead of taking it, however, God's-Gift-To-Women looked up at me and said, "Cover me. And don't forget my feet."

Fortunately, Debbie's "thing" with Larry only lasted three weeks—three weeks in which Tim and I awaited her bulletins as anxiously as any nation listens for the hourly radio reports on the condition of an ailing president or king. We talked it over together, of course—if you could call our series of expostulations a discussion:

"Doesn't she see that he's a pompous ass?"

"How can she stand him?"

"I should have stuffed that blanket in his mouth!"

We never did really discuss it with Debbie. All of our

friends who were in similar **straits counselled in**nocuous comment or silence. As Fred Shultz put it, in his own inimitable, legalistic manner, "When they ask you what you think, they don't really want to know unless it agrees with their own opinion. If you openly oppose them, it only makes them defiant and fires them up straight to where you don't want them to go. The only thing to do is wait and pray that the good sense they must have inherited from you will win out in the end."

This, in general, was the approach to Debbie herself that we adhered to as if it were religious doctrine. In time, happily, as the procession which began in her freshman year continued, we stopped analyzing, even for our own benefit, each character who appeared next, and simply sat back in the prayerful expectation that this, too would pass. And as a rule, it did.

There were some, unquestionably, who gave us a harder time than did the others before the final verdict was in. Tony Amato, for example, had his fraternity pin on Debbie before she suddenly realized what Tim and I could see so plainly (as if it were printed on a big, red neon sign on his face) from the first time he came to our teetotaler home and poured himself a double-Scotch for breakfast, "You know, Mother," said our brilliant daughter, "I've given ₁ my back his pin. I've decided he really drinks too much and I don't think it could work out."

Wally Carter—but for different reasons—was another Rubicon to cross. Wally was a non-person. He never said anything at all on his own, he almost never smiled, and he rarely responded to direct questions with more than a grunt or a shake of his head. How he managed to convey the idea to her remains a mystery to Tim and me, but the fact did emerge most clearly that Wally wanted to marry Debbie. He even produced an engagement ring for her inspection (an ex-girl-friend had returned it two years before) and Debbie, to our horror and amazement, undertook to consider the proposal as if it were a viable proposition.

"Of course I don't love him," she admitted to her father and me. "How can you love someone who doesn't really exist? But I've about made up my mind that I probably won't ever fall in love anyway, so why not settle for Wally?"

Whereupon we told her why not—tactfully, carefully, of course, swallowing our usual dose of the "Hands-Off" medicine that was beginning to taste more and more each day like unadulterated Castor-Oil: she was so young; she *would* find someone to love and be loved by; she would *never* be happy with a husband like Wally; and on and on and on. Thereafter, for three more weeks we hovered between life and death at home while Debbie wrestled with the devil in her dormitory room. When it was over, thank God, and she had regretfully turned her back on that miniature diamond that had dangled before her eyes like a carrot before a hungry horse, her final words were, "Oh well, even if I never do get married, it's nice to know that I did get asked."

In spite of Tony and Wally, though, it was easy come, easy go, on the whole. I came to think of the campus as the Happy Hunting Ground and of the lounge, which was in a large, center building which separated the girls' dormitories from the boys' dormitories, as the Mating Pit. The sofas and easy chairs were invariably pre-empted by sprawling couples so mysteriously and intricately intertwined that it was always embarrassing to have to ask one of them to move over so you could sit down. I never ceased being amazed and intrigued that in the hurried, Houdini-like extrication that followed, all the shifting arms and legs went back into place.

It was to avoid the lounge, particularly, that Debbie brought her conquests home. We, in turn, grateful for the opportunity to inspect, opened our door to her strays: Long-haired, short-haired, bearded, unbearded, Catholic, Protestant, Moslem and Jew. Our home, which in Tim's legal sense was very much our castle even if it were no Buckingham Palace, admitted anyone she had in tow. It became a way of life for all of us and we were growing properly inured—until the whole routine abruptly ended in her sophomore year with the advent of Keane.

Keane Engstrom was big, blond, handsome and intelligent. He was president of the Student Council, president of his fraternity, captain of the basketball team and in love with Debbie. Did Debbie really love him or was she in love with the idea of being loved? We never knew and, in a way, it never mattered. What we had on our hands now was the Great Romance of all time—Romeo and Juliet, Tristan and Isolde notwithstanding.

Weekend after weekend, they came home enveloped in a thick haze that made it harder to make live contact with them than it would have been with the Statue of Liberty. They spent hours looking into each other's eyes and holding hands in the face of bodily movements that sometimes required contortions for them to do so. They had a special song ("Our Song") which they played endlessly and which caused near convulsions anytime they accidentally encountered it. They were so completely unaware of everything and everyone but themselves, that Richard Nixon could have opened a shooting gallery next door, or King Hussein could have been pitching for the Dodgers that season and they wouldn't have known or cared.

redible as it might seem in the face of such intense devotion, Debbie and Keane argued again and again. He had a terrible temper and flared up frequently. If she said hello to another boy, Keane was furious; if he smiled at a girl he knew, Debbie was heartbroken. He came from a sound but poor, blue-collar family and he looked with suspicion and hostility at our professional status. She, in turn, was distressed by his grammatical lapses and minimal manners, and was intent on correcting both before either Tim or I would notice. They planned on marriage, of course, right after graduation, but it was planning that was frequently disrupted by the pattern of their romance: fight and make-up; fight and make-up; fight and make-up.

54

"How can they get married?" Tim asked me worriedly. "If they can't get along harmoniously before, how will they manage after?"

"I know," I agreed despondently. "I like Keane but not as someone for Debbie. It's a mismatch. If you ask me, Debbie just is delighted with her status as the girl friend of the Big Man on the Campus. She's been ripe for a great crush for a long time now. It was bad enough that in high school, anyone who wasn't going steady by the senior year was considered an old maid by the other kids. But in college, you've got to be pinned or get engaged to matter."

"Have you tried talking to her?" Tim persisted. "I know we've always avoided any head-on confrontations, but this is different, don't you think?"

"I've tried, sweetie," I admitted. "But Fred's absolutely right. She won't listen. She doesn't want to hear. She just says I'm spoiling things for her and that I don't really understand how they feel."

At spring recess, Debbie came home on the Thursday of the Easter weekend and Keane was due to arrive that night. His family lived in Oklahoma and it had become custom by then that Keane would visit our place on most school holidays. As soon as Debbie entered the house, however, I could tell something was up.

"Mother," she began excitedly, even before her coat off, "I've made up my mind that I can't marry Keane. We keep fighting and he's so jealous. It's just no use."

To myself I thought: "So what's new?" Aloud, I merely said, "Oh?"

"You can't imagine how awful it's been!" she continued. "We had a bang-up battle yesterday just because I went over some psychology notes with Pete Driscoll. Honestly, Mother, it was humiliating. And I'm through! I'm going to tell Keane as soon as he gets here!"

"As soon as he gets here?" I interrupted my private prayer of gratitude to God to express my horror at her timing. "Debbie, you can't! He'll have to stay the week anyway because he's got no other place to go with his family out of town. Honey, please wait until you're back at school. Don't bring the roof down on all of our Easter. Please!"

"But Mother," Debbie insisted, "I've got to tell him right away. Do you expect me to go on being lovey-dovey with him as if everything were still all right? I know he'll be upset, but so am I, and this way we'll get things squared away before classes start up again. I have to do it as soon as he arrives."

And so she did. The moment Keane came into the house, she led him into the living room and unleashed her atom bomb. Needless to say, Keane erupted like Mt. Vesuvius and Tim and I—as co-inhabitants of the premises—were buried in the debris. There were scenes reminiscent of the climactic finale of an Italian opera. Keane stormed, Debbie wept, Tim and I offered comfort and philosophy—and the full tragedy was acted out on and off during the week.

"I've had it," Tim told me wearily as we deposited the two combatants at their respective dormitories on the next Sunday and started the drive back home.

"Me, too," I agreed, feeling as limp and crumpled as a dishrag that has just emerged from a six-cycle washing machine and been left in a heap to dry. "I can't believe it really happened. Honey," I finished, before dropping off to sleep, propped up against his shoulder, "now we've seen everything. How much more must we take?"

The answer to these famous last words was: One more. Not that we would have balked at even ten more, were it necessary. Parental responsiveness is probably the closest thing to perpetual motion this side of heaven. For myself, although I never understood the whole phenomenon, it has always reinforced my faith in the reliability of God when I realize that even ordinary mortals can never really turn their backs on their children.

In any case, the one more was Pete Driscoll, the young man over whom Debbie and Keane had their last fight. How and why that got started, I don't know, any more than

I could draw the presumption that meeting Pete was all the rope Debbie needed to let Keane go. She did march around with a tragic air for several weeks after the break-up (a suitable mourning period being only proper) but the name of Pete Driscoll began to appear more and more in her conversation. He himself, interestingly enough, did not appear.

This variation in Debbie's usual dating procedure should probably have alerted us to the significance of what was finally happening. But it didn't—and we were totally unprepared for her appearance with Pete one weekend in the early fall of her junior year, and their joint announcement that they were in love and wanted to get married in June. Just like that.

"Married?" Tim gasped.

"In June?" the question was all I could manage.

We looked at Pete the way we would have looked at a Martian—if he had suddenly landed in our midst. Anatomically, he was all there and as we talked, we could not fault his intelligence. But whoever would concede that he was good enough for our daughter?

With true parental astigmatism, therefore, we raised all the traditional objections. Did Debbie and Pete realize that marriage was a serious business? What were they going to live on? What about their education? Were they sure of what they were doing?

The answers were immediately forthcoming and showed full malice of forethought. Pete's father was a Certified Public Accountant. When Pete graduated, he would be going into his father's business. Debbie and he would get married right after final exams, set up housekeeping over the summer, and go through their senior year married.

"It's really simple," Debbie explained. "If you'll just go on with my tuition and my allowance, and if Pete's folks do the same for him, we'll manage fine until graduation. After that, we'll be on easy street, with both of us working. Do you see?"

Tim cleared his throat next and asked as tactfully as he could, "What about it if you do get married and happen to become pregnant?"

Debbie blushed. "Oh, Daddy," she said, "don't be so antidiluvian! Pete and I aren't babies, you know. We believe in planned parenthood. Accidents are really passé."

I cleared my throat then and addressed Pete, "Do your mother and father know about any of this yet? Have they agreed?"

"They're driving down to talk it all out in a few weeks," was his answer. "We live in Ohio—Steubenville. They want to meet Debbie, of course."

"And we," as I told Tim later on when we had collapsed in our bedroom, "must get to meet them! Maybe we can join forces and persuade Debbie and Pete to hold off until after they both graduate. Give themselves more time to be absolutely certain of how they feel."

Accordingly, when Debbie announced, three weeks later, that Pete's parents were due in on Saturday, Tim and I made it our business to accidentally drop by at the same time to see Debbie. What a coincidence! By the same lucky coincidence, we even stayed at the same motel so that by Sunday night, when we said goodby, all of the relevant ground had been covered.

We began slowly and warily, as might be expected, sort of smelling each other out. Then when we were each satisfied that the other couple had neither horns nor tails, we proceeded on to the amenities.

"Debbie's such a lovely girl!"

"Pete is such a fine young man!"

"Isn't it wonderful that they've found each other?"

"Won't they make a nice couple?"

It was a little bit like a polite duel, each side moving forward with a gentle thrust until gradually—by the time Debbie and Pete had said good-night and left us alone—the swordplay ended and we got down to business.

Mr. and Mrs. Driscoll, apparently, were as surprised as

we. Yes, they also wished the children would wait until graduation, but it certainly looked as if their minds were all made up. No, they hadn't raised any objection with Pete because, well, you know how stubborn kids can get when they're crossed (where had we heard that before). And finally, the clincher: after all, it could be worse; what if we said no and they went ahead and shacked up?

Maybe it was the Driscoll logic. Maybe it was plain, acute emotional exhaustion from Keane and all of his predecessors. Maybe it was that Pete seemed wonderfully endowed to us in the light of Larry and Tony Amato. Whatever: In June, at the end of their junior year, Debbie and Pete were married.

Mothers of the Bride are always supposed to cry at their daughter's wedding. I sobbed the night before the wedding in the privacy of our bedroom: She was so young; she was still like a little girl; should we really have aided and abetted her in this? Could it really be happening that Debbie was getting married? Where, oh where had all the years gone?

The day of the wedding, I was calm, collected and numb. I sat in my pew reviewing all the arrangements I had so carefully made for the reception to follow the ceremony, much the way Eisenhower must have examined his preparations for the invasion of Europe. When the organ sounded forth at the end of the service, and a radiant Mr. and Mrs. Peter Driscoll started down the aisle, a feeling of unadulterated exhilaration swept over me.

For better or worse, we had done it! For better or worse, it was over!

Oh, moment sublime, never again to be attained! Because, in fact, nothing was over. Marrying off Debbie was merely opening the door on the road to grandparenthood. Which, from a parental point of view, was merely one more step from the frying pan into the fire.

Chapter IV

THE ORIGIN OF THE SPECIES

EXCEPT for the fact of our birth, grandparenthood is probably almost the only state of adult being that is thrust upon us without our permission or concurrence. We choose a husband; we decide on a child; we become a doctor, lawyer or Indian Chief. Only on the grandparent level are we suddenly and arbitrarily informed of what has been done to us after there is no undoing it.

This physiological truth, however, is but symbolic of the larger, more important, elemental and painful principle that all grandparents must learn to accept early on, if they are to make a satisfactory adjustment to grandparent life. To wit: that no matter how much we may be emotionally and deeply affected by the advent of that first grandchild, *it is still not our baby.* We may follow the pregnancy along inch by inch, with more concern than the attending obstetrician, and we may even foot the bills—but when all is said and done, we are merely invited guests at someone else's party.

Naturally, this kind of revelation is not given to grandparents through any cataclysmic, divine intervention. Nor is it a message that is preached from most of the magazine pulpits in the land. Intimations of it can be glimpsed throughout the currently popular "Don't interfere," parent-child theology, but it is so commingled with the rest that it comes through like a congregation Speaking in Tongues.

For myself, the learning process was—as all my grandparental learning processes are—slow. And I can only say, without either rationalization or self justification, "How could it be any other way?"

To begin with, the record must clearly show by now that grandparenthood was as far from my mind after Debbie's marriage as the mating habits of the Drosophila Fruit Fly. Debbie and Pete were both still in the student category, and one of the implied conditions in our agreement to underwrite their marital enterprise was that reproduction was no part of the deal—at least in the immediate future. I say "implied" because the subject had never been discussed in depth or signed in blood.

"Do you think they're really briefed on contraception?" I had asked Tim worriedly, as the wedding date drew near.

"Have you talked any to Debbie about it?" he had asked right back—obviously unwilling to commit himself.

I hate conversations that are a series of questions, but Tim and I had enough rapport between us so that we could always automatically fill in the unspoken, connecting sentences.

"Should I?" the interrogation went on.

"Would they mind?" Tim had had the last question.

"I think they would," I had finally become positive. "I know I minded all the talk I had to listen to when we were getting married. It was obnoxious."

Indeed, the memory of some of those pre-nuptial sermons Tim and I sat through still rankles—although they should be considered the natural by-product of the twentieth century sexual revolution. Now that sex has been taken out of the bedroom and been plunked down in the kitchen and parlor, the physical side of marriage is no longer a private affair. It has been added to the list of public concerns along with the national debt and unemployment insurance. It has changed marriage from a loving art to a scientific, laborious undertaking. Textbooks on married love that sometimes look like an elementary course in biological reproduction and whose writers seem to assume that the genitalia are never discovered until their books are read, sit on more living room shelves these days than does the Bible.

In any case, with our own experiences in mind, neither Tim nor I could bring ourselves to put any segment of the subject on the family agenda. Instead, we both reminded ourselves encouragingly that "Hadn't Debbie herself mentioned something about Planned Parenthood?" Besides which, everybody knows that today's youngsters start learning about sex back in kindergarten and probably are more knowledgeable by the time they enter their teens than Masters and Johnson!

It was a comforting presumption, however fallacious. In blissful but short-lived confidence, we never even recognized the existence of such a concept as grandparenthood, and concentrated only on the ramifications of helping Debbie and Pete get settled in their little apartment. Which concentration, eventually, merely reinforced our fond and foolish belief that Debbie married was still Debbie our daughter—a handicap that made the subsequent plunge into grandparenthood all the more difficult to take.

We began Debbie's marriage, unfortunately, with no apparent, outward differences that set one state apart from the other. Whereas before, for instance, we had fixed up a dormitory room for her, we were now engaged upon furnishing a one-bedroom flat. The project was much bigger, of course, but so much more fun that most of the more serious significances in the homesteading for this new family were lost upon us.

Interestingly enough, it was not a desire for involvement as such that got us involved initially; it was merely a natural, instinctive, parental response to a child's need for help. Had we ever refused any S.O.S. from Debbie before she was married?

Accordingly, exactly two weeks after the wedding, when Debbie and Pete were due back at their place after their honeymoon (courtesy of Mr. and Mrs. Driscoll, Senior), Tim and I undertook a trek thence that would have qualified us to join any Wagon Train that ever set forth in the history of the United States. You see, all the wedding presents had already made our home look like a Discount Warehouse on the day of the Big Sale, and there didn't seem any way to reclaim our ownership of the premises in the foreseeable future unless we delivered the stuff ourselves. Besides which, Debbie had merely asked worriedly, in the midst of the wedding festivities, "Oh, Mother, how will we ever get these things to our apartment?" And I had automatically responded, "Don't fret, honey. Your father and I will manage somehow."

"Somehow" was right. We put the dinette table on top of the car legs up, and tied it on like a dead deer; four chairs, a big mirror, two bookcases, a set of dishes, silver, glassware, linens, a toaster, an electric can-opener and an assortment (many in duplicate) of pewter and silver household items were fitted into the back seat area and into the trunk which remained open. Obviously there was no rear visibility, and I functioned as Tim's navigator, when necessary, by going halfway out the side window to look behind for him. N... . say .iore?

It was a memorable and hazardous two-hour trip. Tim kept complaining most of the time. "We must be crazy," was one frequent comment. "We'll get killed," was another; and his final masterpiece, as we pulled into the parking lot on our arrival, was, "Greater love hath no parent than that he would lay. down his life to bring his child her wedding presents."

Having brought the presents, however, it was almost inevitable that we should stay to help arrange them. Especially since we were asked.

Actually it was mostly Debbie and I who ran around pushing and pulling to get the most striking effects. For females, the instinct to play house is as inherent as the law of self-preservation, and as basic as holding hands in the movies. It begins with the first new doll and the little, next-door neighbor boy, and it never ends. But just as the neighbor boy is often an unwilling participant in the "Now I'll be the Mamma and you be the Daddy and this is our home" routine, so, too, is the adult male a reluctant accessory to the game. A man lives in his house, he sleeps in his house, he eats in his house. He covers the floors when he thinks of it, lights the lamps, when necessary, and draws the shades; but rarely is it more than a type of required shelter, a means to a utilitarian end. And never, never does he wholly comprehend the frills and fancies of housekeeping that are so vital and endearing to the feminine heart.

With and without Tim and Pete, therefore, this first weekend was followed by many others in which we all—in varying degrees—helped Debbie decorate her place. Poor Debbie was so full of enthusiasm and ideas that it was impossible just to stand aside and let her flounder on alone. She had absolute confidence in any magazine that promised Voodoo results from bright colors and small prints and tiny rooms—and she was ready to try it all.

"Can't you just see the bedroom in pale blue?" she said one Saturday, introducing us to her cans of blue paint.

"What do you think of this beautiful wallpaper pattern?" she asked a few weeks later, unveiling another purchase.

Debbie always made it sound as if papering and painting were as simple as brushing one's teeth. She even had a magazine article to prove her point (ah, the perfidy of those magazines), "Anyone Can Paint a Room the Easy Way."

So, at her behest, we painted and we papered and it was definitely *not* easy. What the magazines didn't tell us was that paint drips—all over the painter. That when you wield a brush, small rivulets of paint roll down and ruin the smooth surface of the wall. That reaching up and down and up and down and up and down makes your arm feel as if it's attached to a dead weight, which will sooner or later detach it from your body. That painting is messy and dirty and sticky; that it clings to your hair and your hands and your clothes. That the odor of paint is unbearable, and that it makes it difficult to breathe and causes the eyes to smart and run.

As for wallpapering, I can only say we were equally betrayed. Debbie had not bought pre-pasted and pre-trimmed paper because "that would have cost more money" and besides (for wallpapering we were following directions in a book), it said right there that it was simple to make up some paste.

So we made some paste.

"It's too thin," Tim, who was doing the mixing, said.

"Add some more flour," Pete suggested.

"More flour coming up," I answered, dumping it in.

"Now it's too thick," Tim said, pouring in some more water.

Finally, it seemed just of the right consistency, only quite lumpy.

"Does it talk about lumps in the book?" I asked Debbie.

"Yes," she said, flipping the pages until she found the exact spot.

"What does it say?" I spoke anxiously.

"To watch out for them," she read the paragraph aloud. "Oh well, let's no ___ ___ about ___ ___'s cut the paper."

Since we had no p..per ___ ___ ___ we cut the long strips on the floor, which was uncomfortable, at best, and inaccurate, at worst. Then we hung the paper and discovered that the paste did show through as bumps from underneath. What's more, we promptly realized that we had not been too successful in matching the designs on the different pieces each to each so that occasionally the lady in the print was to be seen holding a house instead of a bunch of flowers.

"So what?" Debbie exclaimed, as we stood back when most of our work was done. "I think it's beautiful!"

She really did—and in a way, so did I. There was a wonderful feeling of accomplishment, of having hewn a home out of a wilderness. There was also, however, an entirely misleading feeling of togetherness, as if we were one family instead of two.

Tim recognized this pitfall before I did and brought me to a sudden halt. "Edwina," he said one Sunday, when we were driving back home after our usual cooperative efforts on behalf of the newlyweds, "I think we've done enough. They can get by on their own from here on in. Classes will be starting soon and they can use all the time they can get to be alone and make their adjustments to each other now. Do you know what I mean?"

I knew. Not that I had ever been too worried about Debbie and Pete as a couple. There may never have been a lot of drippy goo holding them together, but the sincerity of their relationship had always seemed to possess most of the solid elements needed to weld any boy and girl into a husband and wife. At least, I fervently hoped so!

My concern—such as it was—stemmed mostly from the overall attitude towards marriage in the world around. Too many people nowadays regard marriage as impermanent as a fur coat: Something to be discarded or worn at will from season to season. There is a spreading attitude that seems to hold that spouse, as need be, can be changed as casually and regularly as a man changes his socks—and the need compelling a marital change can range all the way from a disagreement over broccoli for dinner to a new lover. In the words of one well-known woman celebrity whose discarded spouses could have formed their own hockey team, and with whom I shared a lecture platform on the subject one afternoon, "How can anyone object to divorces and remarriages? Would you interfere with our right to search for happiness?"

In view of all of which, therefore, I responded to Tim's remarks somewhat anxiously. "Don't you think Debbie and Pete are getting along well together?" I asked, pushing myself upright on the car seat. "Don't you? I do."

Naturally, there had been some days when Tim and I could sense that we had arrived at the Driscoll ménage smack in the middle of what must have been a major domestic controversy before the doorbell rang. It was obvious that they had automatically ceased arguing at the sound—like the sudden dispersal of sidewalk brawlers at the approach of a police siren. Debbie would be looking at Pete in a "Who is this strange man?" tone of voice; and Pete would be glaring back as if he were Rhett Butler in the later scenes of "Gone With the Wind"; while Tim and I would make lots of small talk, pretending desperately that the whole thing was an apparition.

None of this, however, had seriously disturbed me. After all, Debbie and Pete seemed to be happy most of the time. Besides, as any veteran of the connubial arena must surely know, there are bound to be times in any marriage when even divorce seems nowhere near as appropriate as plain murder. Truly, modern marriage is the most unhonored miracle of modern times. It is probably the only voluntary human relationship where two people, two separate, discordant entities, cheerfully set out to balance a social, physiological and psychological budget that makes the national one seem as easy to balance as kindergarten arithmetic—and often succeed. More significantly, it is also the only field of human activity, beginning with the Battle of Jericho and ending with the Battle Sessions of the United Nations, where human beings have ever even seriously tried.

"Now don't start getting into a stew about that pair," Tim hurried to reassure me, keeping his eyes on the road while he reached blindly with one hand for mine. "They're doing fine. Some spots, sure enough, but certainly every bit as well as can be expected for a newly married couple."

I laughed at his wording. Then I agreed, "I know. But sweetie, the trouble is that people don't realize that while a mutual love of Bach and a kindred loathing of Gertrude Stein may make the genesis of a very satisfactory courtship,

68

they do not necessarily insure a fine marriage. In wedlock, it's the big things that count most, like: 'Why isn't my suit back yet from the cleaners?' or 'What did you do with the twenty dollars I gave you yesterday?' and 'Fish again? Oh God!' It can be more painful than breaking in a pair of tight, new shoes—and it takes a lot longer."

"Which is exactly what I was talking about," Tim replied. "Let's relax and let them do the same. I've had enough of setting out almost every Saturday like a union man reporting in for a piece-work job. Debbie's got her own life with Pete now, but more important, let's you and me reclaim ours. Remember me? I'm your husband."

"You'd better be!" I squeezed his hand hard. "And you're absolutely right. We've spent years centering our lives to a large extent on growing Debbie up and getting her settled. But thank God, that's done now. We can really be free again to do our own thing!"

The idea had a lovely sound and it was lovely for all of about four months. We still heard from Debbie of course, fairly regularly. She and Pete made a few weekend trips home on a scavenger hunt to find and then requisition any and all available household furnishings that Tim and I could spare from our place for theirs: old dining room curtains, a pair of wooden candlesticks, some china figurines, odd throw pillows, et cetera. School had opened on schedule, and both of them were happily eking out their senior year exactly as they had planned.

"Isn't it wonderful?" I asked Tim one evening when we were luxuriating in a quiet nothingness at home. "I don't wait for the telephone the way I used to. I just can take it for granted that if Debbie didn't show up after classes, Pete would be bound to know. Honestly, darling, a student could vanish from one of those dormitory rooms and no one would miss her for days and days. She could drop dead in her own bed, and who would care? I kind of waited from phone call to phone call just to be reassured that Debbie was still alive."

"What I like," Tim added his own bit, "is the absolute freedom to come and go as we like and that your focus is more on us. Do you know that there were many nights when you wouldn't leave the house because Debbie hadn't called and you were afraid you'd miss it if we left?"

As I said, it was lovely—until Christmas.

Christmas had always been a very special time in my life, but this Christmas seemed even more so to me because it was the first since Debbie's marriage. Carried away by a heady feeling of holiday spirit and exhilaration, I polished the silver as if I were polishing jewels for Tiffany's, cleaned, scrubbed and wound up issuing wholesale invitations for an Open House on Christmas Eve (the night Debbie and Pete were due to arrive) to celebrate. By the appointed hour, the lamps in the house were all lit, the stereo was turned on low with some soft, sweet background music, the Christmas tree was a shining brightness in the front hall and there were big, white chrysanthemums in a crystal vase on the black piano. I was filled with a strange, excited expectation—like before the curtain goes up on a Broadway first night—and I felt ready for anything.

"Anything" turned out to be Debbie and Pete's announcement that they were going to have a baby. It was made at six o'clock—two minutes after they pulled into the driveway, and exactly thirty minutes before the first guest arrived.

"Mother! Daddy!" Debbie spoke even while she was pulling off her coat. "Guess what? I'm pregnant!"

Tim and I stopped dead in our tracks.

"Pregnant?" I repeated, as if she had said something in a foreign language I didn't understand.

"I'm going to have a baby," she amplified impatiently. "In July. I just found out yesterday. I thought we'd wait and tell you in person—when we got here."

"Oh." It was all I could say.

I looked at both of them: Debbie wore an expression of pleased importance; Pete looked very much the way the whale must have looked after he swallowed down Jonah. Question after question flooded my brain: Is it an accident? Didn't you know any better? What about your Planned Parenthood? Why couldn't you have waited until graduation? But there was nothing I could really ask. Marriage is always a private affair and Debbie was a married woman— far removed from the daughter of whom I could have demanded indignantly and rightfully, "How did you break that cookie jar?"

Tim recovered first. "In July?" he asked, and I could almost hear him counting up the months. Then, obviously relieved, he said, "But what about your school? You're supposed to graduate in June. Are you going to forfeit your degree for just a few months?"

"Oh no, sir," Pete answered for Debbie. "She'll go on with classes all the way through. When we graduate, we'll move to Steubenville. I'll start work with my father and Debbie will have the baby there. We'll be settled by then, so there'll be no problem."

"But won't you be showing a lot by June?" I asked next, still essentially stunned and able to function only the way a worm goes on wiggling after it's dead. "You know, pregnancy can't be concealed."

"Good grief!" Debbie spoke with annoyance. "This isn't the Middle Ages, Mother. People don't hide pregnancies these days. And we are married!" Then her eyes clouded up and she was almost crying. "I knew you'd be surprised," she lamented, "but I did think you'd be glad for both of us. You're spoiling the whole thing. You never even said 'Congratulations!' "

Obviously, Debbie could not ever begin to understand our point of view, much less accept the fact that we were entitled to one. The wall between the generations, unfortunately, is more impermeable than that between this world and the next. Wherefore, there was nothing more to say or do except to join in like a computerized robot in shaking hands with Pete, putting my arms around Debbie, and assuring both of them that although we were definitely shocked, we were also pleased.

Happily, the first guest arrived in the middle of this theatrical performance and the subject had to give way to the escalating party. Tim and I became busily involved—but alas, not diverted—in greeting visitors, passing trays of food and punch and adding to the mountain-sized pile of coats and scarves that was growing on our bed. Once, in a trip to the kitchen, I bumped into Tim and asked him frantically as if we were continuing a private conversation, "I just can't believe it, Honey! How could it have happened?" To which Tim, without even looking up from the bowl of nuts he was filling, tersely replied, "The usual way."

I tried to be a proper hostess, but even I could sense that my smile was forced, and that I was functioning more on the level of a night watchman on a job or a head-waiter at a society party. It came as no surprise to me, therefore, that about nine-thirty, when only a few close friends were left, and Debbie and Pete had gone off to say "Hi" to one of her old girlfriends, and Tim and I had collapsed on the sofa, that Chris Keryokis, who was Debbie's godfather, interrupted the waning conversation and asked, "What's the matter with you two anyway? You haven't been yourselves all evening."

With everyone looking at us expectantly, Tim turned to me for silent corroboration and then said, "Edwina and I and Pete are going to have a baby. It's a real blockbuster for us, you know, since we had assumed that they would at least hold off until they were out of college."

Fred Shultz, who was one of those present, asked next, "When's the big event?"

"In July," I spoke defensively.

Fred calculated mentally. "For heaven's sake," he exploded with laughter, "at least it's well within the legal time limit. Count your blessings. Our Lucy went to the altar seven months on the way."

Someone else came up with, "So you're going to be a grandma and grandpa! Welcome to the club!"

Chris spoke last. "Why should you be surprised at Debbie's becoming pregnant?" he asked. "I could have told you so from the beginning. If you give little children matches to play with, they'll get burned. You should have known."

Well, we knew now and there was nothing for us to do but adjust to the general idea. The brief, beautiful hiatus during which we had tucked Debbie comfortably away in the back of our concerns was over. Once again, life had demonstrated to me that nothing lasts: Is your bank account budgeted? The baby gets sick. Do you like your house? The taxes are raised. There is no escaping.

Christmas, of course, floundered on from its inauspicious beginning. When Debbie and Pete left at the end of the week, so did our peace of mind. For example, just as they were about to go out the front door, Debbie happened to mention that she was really enjoying working in radiology at the hospital this semester. She mentioned it casually, pleasantly, as if she were talking about a course in art appreciation, but Tim and I took off like space rockets to the moon.

"Radiology?" Tim gasped, his voice growing louder with each sentence. "And you pregnant?"

"You mean you're exposing yourself to X-rays?" I asked, approaching my own crescendo, like a mezzo-soprano reaching for high C. "Debbie, it's dangerous for you and the baby. You have to switch services. Tell them you're pregnant."

"Oh, I'll see," Debbie answered evasively. "I hate to stand out like a sore thumb."

"You'll see?" Tim thundered. "Young lady, if you don't ask to change over to something else, and tell them why, I'll go down there myself and take care of it!"

Fortunately, Debbie knew Tim was not making any idle threat, so she agreed, although reluctantly, to comply with

73

our request. Nevertheless, our feeling of calm and confidence in her management of the entire proceedings was permanently thereafter undermined. It was, in a way, our first intimation of the secondary role which all grandparents play in the grandparental process; and even in this early stage, before Melinda was an accomplished fact, it was a difficult adjustment to make.

We worried on and off, consequently, throughout the long months of Debbie's pregnancy. Did she have morning sickness? We never got a straight answer. Was she getting enough rest? Don't be silly, Mother. How was the obstetrics ward to which she'd been switched? It's a breeze. Was she on her feet too much? "Too much for what?" she wanted to know. "Varicosities?" we timidly suggested. "Good God," she replied.

From the very beginning of her pregnancy, Debbie made it very plain in every possible way that Melinda was strictly her show. Oh, she welcomed the crib we brought when she and Pete talked about having to put the baby in a dresser drawer because they didn't have the money to buy one. She was delighted with the folding carriage and the tiny infant clothes. We even enjoyed several shopping excursions for maternity dresses at that point where she literally burst through a closed zipper on a skirt she was trying to squeeze into. But there was always a line that I dared not cross.

"I swear, Tim," I told him forlornly one day shortly before Debbie's graduation, "I feel like a yoyo at the end of a string. What does she want anyway? If I don't act interested and excited about the baby, she gets hurt. If I do, she pulls back as if I'm going to steal her candy. She's never been like this before."

"It's just the next phase of the maturing process," Tim tried to console me. "She's got a lot of adjusting to do."

"Well, so do I," I complained. "Why are people only concerned with the adjustments of the young? Parents have their adjustments to make all along the way, too, but no one gives a hoot. Is Debbie no longer supposed to be my child just because she's having one of her own?"

"Honey," Tim put his arms around me as he spoke, "I don't know the answers, either. I've got my adjustments also. Do you know how it makes me feel to see my Debbie all swollen up and distorted by pregnancy?"

"The way I feel," I replied promptly. "Everytime I see Debbie in her advanced pregnancy state, I have to swallow hard. Somehow, I guess in parental minds, our children are always slim, trim and graceful, gliding along with the exuberance and beauty of youth forever. It's how we think of them and how we want them to be—free even of the burdens of their own making."

"Well," Tim said, letting me go and picking up his attaché case to leave for the office, "just remember that this burden is entirely of her own making. It's her baby, honey, not yours."

"I know," I said, walking with him to the door. "Only, I used to think grandparents have some peripheral rights in the baby, too."

"And now you know better." Tim kissed me good-by.

But I didn't really know better yet; not, that is, until Melinda was born.

Debbie's general attitude, obviously, was the kind of elementary clue even Sherlock Holmes' Dr. Watson would have recognized. I saw it, of course, but it was like glimpsing the picture in a jigsaw puzzle before all the pieces were in place.

Naming the baby was another message that I read but never fully decoded. It began with Debbie's announcement over the telephone that she and Pete were thinking of calling the baby Priscilla, if it were a girl, and Cyril, if it were a boy.

Almost without thinking, and as instinctively as one shuts one's eyes to avoid a foreign body from coming in, I reacted with horror. "Cyril?" I exclaimed. "Where'd you get that one from? And Priscilla—oh honey, there was a Prissy in my class in high school and I just hated her. I couldn't bear

75

to call any baby I cared about by that name! The associations are just awful."

There was a cold, blank silence on the line. Then Debbie spoke, "You know, Mother, this is my baby and Pete's. We can name him or her whatever we want."

It couldn't have been said more plainly, although the blast was tempered by Debbie's immediate conciliatory remark that she would prefer to choose a name that we and Pete's family would like. Still, after that, if she had decided on Gargantua the Great, I would have said nothing.

The feeling of alienation, of being the outsider looking in, was climaxed by the birth of Melinda. We had dutifully attended Debbie's graduation ceremonies, albeit with a secret sigh of relief that she had made it to the finishing line. In her jaunty cap and flowing gown, I heard someone watching her go by in the procession say to someone else, "Is she or isn't she?" but the humor in the situation was somehow lost on Tim and me in the strangeness we both felt by then in the whole situation.

It was a strangeness, however, that seemed to become unimportant and irrelevant the moment Pete called one Thursday morning in late July to tell us that Debbie had gone into labor. They had moved to Steubenville by then, only an hour away, but in view of the overall way I had come to feel, I asked Pete before setting out, "Does Debbie want me to come?"

"She wants you to come." He sounded nervous and breathless.

Then followed the longest, hardest eight-hour wait I had ever endured in my whole life—a wait compounded by the fact that I was not permitted to go in and see Debbie.

"Only the husband can go inside the labor room," the nurse on the floor told me in a harsh tone of voice, as if there were brass knuckles on her tongue.

"But I'm her Mother!" I protested, briefly forgetting that in this affair, that didn't matter.

"Only the husband." She repeated her litany and

marched off like a top sergeant at the head of a firing squad.

I sat. I fumed. I worried. I prayed, oh how I prayed, "Please God, it's Debbie in there. Just take care of her and see that everything's all right. I'll never gripe again about anything."

It was the usual racketeering spirit that pervades most prayer—the kind of religious bargaining with God that goes, "Make Jane better and I'll stop playing the races," or, "Fix up my leg, and I'll never take another drink." But I meant it.

At one point, I did sneak back into Debbie's room when Pete came out to make one of his regular reports. She was dripping with perspiration and crying with pain. "Oh, Mother," she gripped my hand till it hurt, "I can't bear it! I'll die before it's over!"

Tears filled my eyes, but before I could utter a word, the militant nurse discovered me and led me away as if I were a bank robber caught in the act. She should have been with the F.B.I.!

"But honey," Tim tried to comfort me in one of my frequent calls to his office, "you know first babies take long in coming. Would it help any if I closed shop and drove down?"

"No." I knew he was working on an important case. "You couldn't do anything either. Just pray."

Finally, at five-thirty in the afternoon, a weak and exhausted-looking Pete came out to tell me that they were wheeling Debbie into the delivery room.

"It won't be long now," he said.

I nodded, settling back for my final vigil as he walked away.

At six-fifteen, Pete came dashing up the hall, looking for all the world like the "After" part of a Geritol ad.

"It's a girl! It's a girl!" He was beside himself with excitement.

"Debbie?" I asked.

"Wonderful! Perfect!" I had never seen him so exuberant before. "Just stand here. They'll roll her out on a bed in just a minute. Look! Here she comes!"

I stood as told because I could not move. Loud hosannahs echoed through my soul as the hospital bed on casters came slowly down the hallway with Debbie in it, cradling a small bundle in her arm. I tried to get over to one side to see the baby, but Pete got there first. I reached up on my toes, trying to look over his shoulder as he bent forward to kiss Debbie.

Briefly, I glimpsed a pair of big, clear, beautiful, blue eyes that watched us all with interest as if to say? "And where am I now?" As briefly, I caught a fleeting look at Debbie's radiant smile as she held Melinda close and asked Pete, almost with awe: "Can you believe that this wonderful creature was really inside me all that time? And that now she's ours? Can you believe that this is our very own baby?"

Quietly, contentedly, I turned aside. Yes, in many ways, a grandparent is an outsider. This was—and had always been—Debbie's baby all the way through: Debbie's and Pete's. I had waited for her and I had prayed for her, but she was not mine.

I didn't like the feel of that fact any more than I ever had. There was something about it that seemed inherently unfair: to be so much a part of something in which you had no part!

For that moment, though, none of it mattered. I would undoubtedly quibble with it all over and over again later on. I would probably even never fully understand it. But for that little while, at least, the miracle of birth transcended everything else. I could rejoice with all my heart in my child's joy—and be temporarily deluded into thinking that that was enough.

Chapter V

AFTER THE BALL

MODERN grandparents, in a general sense, are as emasculated as Liberace and as uncommunicative as the Mona Lisa. Their most outstanding characteristic is a remarkable ability to be seen but not heard—an affliction which society used to reserve for the very young, but which has now become the rock upon which proper grandparenthood is built. They may hear but never jeer; they may acclaim but never proclaim.

Of course, it might be said that this kind of expertise is a natural outgrowth of modern parenthood which often had many of the same earmarks. We struggle through our children's growth from adolescence onward with a Non-Interference Policy that we adhere to like alcoholics undergoing enforced water-cures. But the self-imposed speechlessness of grandparenthood makes all of the prior restraint seem as uninhibited as a rock festival.

My own baptism by total immersion into this aspect of grandparenthood was almost immediate. My adjustment to the whole concept, however, was never really or wholeheartedly achieved—then and to this day.

I arrived home on the evening of Melinda's birth feeling somewhat the way the three Wise Men must have felt after they had left the stable: a mixture of relief, exhilaration, fulfillment and exhaustion. Even Tim was so much impressed by my reaction that he listened patiently to my blow by blow account with no show of his customary intolerance for such trivia.

"Well," he said, when I had finally unwound, like a top that has stopped spinning, "thank God all went well. Now tell me this, honey: Do you realize that we have become a set of grandparents?"

"In name only." I smiled at him wearily. "It takes time to get the feel of it. Right now, it's like a label on a can, and has no significance until and unless the contents actually correspond to the description. You know—it's sort of like a driver's permit to operate a car: it says you may but it doesn't mean you can. Anyway," I concluded, with a big yawn, "how can you be a grandfather yet when you haven't even seen her?"

"Come to bed, darling." Tim pulled me up from my chair. "We'll drive over to the hospital Saturday and pay our proper respects. I'd go tomorrow—except for this case I'm working on. It can't wait."

On Saturday morning, therefore, we headed for the hospital early enough to arrive by ten o'clock, when visiting hours began. Although I had spoken to Debbie on the phone on Friday and knew everything was fine, I was filled with excitement and eagerness and kept hurrying Tim down the long corridor to Debbie's room. When we knocked, however, there was no answer.

"Are you looking for Mrs. Driscoll?" a passing nurse asked Tim and me. "She went home this morning. Her husband came in about seven o'clock and she signed herself out. Took the baby, too."

"Oh. Thank you." I felt bewildered. "Was anything wrong?"

"Not at all," the nurse replied, starting to move away. "They just decided to go."

Without even the need for any spoken word, Tim and I headed for the car and Debbie's home. As we were driving along, however, my sense of outrage exploded like a volcanic eruption.

"They just decided to go!" I exclaimed. "With a two-day-old infant and no one to help! They must be crazy!"

"Take it easy," Tim warned, keeping his eyes fixed on the road. "You're getting all ready to let Debbie have it and you know you can't."

"Why can't I?" I demanded belligerently.

"Because you can't. Because it's her baby and she can do as she pleases." Then his voice softened and he went on, almost gently, "Honey, I thought you had made your peace with this fact that night Melinda was born. Remember? We were the outsiders looking in, but it was O.K. because you liked what you were looking at: Debbie's happiness."

"Well, I' don't like what I'm looking in at now," I replied grumpily. "But don't worry. I've had years of training. I'll hold my peace."

It was a noble resolution but not an easy one to keep as that memorable first day of practical grandparenthood wore on. I began well enough by walking into Debbie and Pete's apartment with brazen nonchalance, as if every new mother dragged herself and her new baby home from the hospital thirty-six hours after birth.

"I got fed up with all that hospital routine," Debbie told us with equal casualness as we entered. "It's so restrictive. So I called Pete and told him to come and take us home."

Tim and I both nodded agreeably.

Then Debbie continued: "How do I look? I've just about managed to squeeze into my old girdle, but I guess I've got a lot of pounds to take off yet, don't you think?"

I thought exactly what I had always thought and exactly what I had tried in vain to tell Debbie for all those months. Strict dietary limitations are vital in pregnancy if one is to wind up afterwards with any kind of a figure comparable to the one that existed before. Somehow, the weight gained sticks to one's anatomy like taffy, and looks like lumpy stuffing in a Teddy bear. What takes nine months to put on can take ninety months to take off.

Again, however, I just smiled pleasantly and made some noncommittal noises. It was Tim who came through with the necessary diversionary tactics.

"You look great, honey," he told Debbie cheerfully. "Now, where did you hide that baby? Don't I get to see her?"

We all trooped into the small bedroom and gathered around the crib as if at the unveiling of a masterpiece. Tim, who had never even had a glimpse of Melinda before, leaned over in an effort to look more carefully at her sleeping face.

"Don't strain, Daddy," Debbie said. "I'll pick her up for you. You're only getting a peek."

As she started to lift the infant, I found myself suddenly unable to keep still—although I should have known better.

"Debbie," I exclaimed, "don't disturb that child. Your father can see her when you give her her next feeding. When will that be?"

By this time, of course, Debbie had Melinda in her arms and was trying—to my horror—to make her wake up and open her eyes. After a few minutes of unsuccessful manipulation, she put her down and answered me, "What do you mean by her next feeding time? It's whenever she cries."

"Oh. You're using Self-Demand." It was not a question, but a simple statement of fact.

"Definitely." Debbie made it sound as unalterable as the correct answer to an arithmetic problem. And this time I did not err—especially since Tim caught my eye and winked.

There was no point in even opening up any discussion about infant feeding methods, which I had personally seen vary through the years as repeatedly and pointlessly as hemline lengths on ladies' dresses: For myself, I had decided that adherence to a schedule with a baby was the only way to preserve maternal sanity and prevent family martyrdom. As far as I could ever determine, Self-Demand was probably practiced by the Neanderthals; and it certainly must have been what Grandma used when, with a dozen or more children to do for, the newest was likely to be neglected until he made himself heard. Besides, even if one could cope in a Self-Demand way with one child, with two or three or more children in one family self-demanding themselves at the same time all over the place, life in Alcatraz during a prison break would be infinitely more peaceful.

Fortunately, Debbie interpreted my lack of comment as some kind of assent. "I'm also breast feeding, you know," she went on self-importantly, "with supplemental bottles." She paused as Melinda—in a belated response to all the poking—began to cry. "Oh, there she goes. Would you all please leave the room? Not you, Pete. You'll stay and help me, won't you, dear?"

"Humpf!" I grunted to Tim, as he and I obediently marched back into the living room. "She's sure feeling her Cheerios, isn't she? It was bad enough to endure in silence when she was pregnant, but how will I bear it now that she's shifted into high gear?"

Tim knew exactly what I meant. Debbie's attitude throughout the nine months had been all that both of us had always deplored in women who were expecting their first child. She had walked with the proud, self-conscious waddle peculiar to those carrying their first-born; she had sat as if right in the most comfortable chair in any room; she had worn the most suggestive maternity clothes from the second month onward; and had had all the urges, desires and privileges belonging unto her condition. We had tried to laugh about it privately before, but we had been buttressed then by the obviously unfounded hope that it would soon pass.

"Come on, honey," Tim almost whispered his reply, "she's only just starting out. Give her time to settle down. You know as well as I that there's no point in saying anything anyway."

I knew. I just didn't understand. If our grown children are entitled to their freedom of action—and they are—why can't they co-exist at least with their parents' equal rights to freedom of speech? Even Russia hears us out before she proceeds to do as she pleases.

In the midst of my silent reflections on this subject, Debbie came in and sat down with us.

"She wouldn't take anything." she said.

"When did she have a feeding last?" I asked, trying not to sound disturbed.

"At six-thirty this morning." Debbie seemed utterly exhausted. "And it's eleven-thirty now."

"Why don't you lie down for a bit?" I suggested. "Maybe I can give her a bottle in a little while."

"No. I want to breast feed as much as I can." Debbie closed her eyes and leaned back in her chair.

"Honey," Pete stood over her worriedly. "Should I go out and get some Pampers? And some food? And what else?"

"Where's your diaper stack?" I asked, remembering that Pete's parents were gifting them with six months of the service.

"Oh, Mother," Debbie spoke with her eyes still shut tightly, "you're forgetting that we came home early. The first delivery will be on Monday. And that's when Lillie is starting also."

Lillie was the part-time maid Debbie had hired to help out after the baby came. It suddenly hit me that the whole place was an incredible mess. The living room was dwarfed with the presence of the big, shiny baby carriage. The kitchen, where we had gathered earlier, was filled to the brim with a baby bathinette in the middle, and with towels and diapers even hanging from cupboard doors, like banners in a United Nations meeting hall.

Almost instinctively, I took the next step in my grandparenthood without even realizing I was doing so. There may be strict censorship in the verbal area, but there is never any restriction whatsoever on a grandparent's contribution to the grubby chores that a grandchild imposes.

"Sweetie," I said, standing up and going over to Tim, "why don't you and Peter go out for all the necessaries? I'll make up a list. And you Debbie, just stretch out on the sofa and relax. I'll straighten up around here so that we can have some lunch."

The idea of specific action pleased everyone. Tim and Pete left promptly, Debbie lay down as directed, and I tackled the cleaning. The baby carriage, for example, was pushed into the farthest corner of the hallway, and Debbie's suitcase was moved into her bedroom. After some dusting and neatening, I progressed to the kitchen. There the bathinette was folded up and placed against the side wall, all the scattered paraphernalia was gathered, sorted and disposed of either in the trash, the laundry basket or put into an orderly arrangement. Then the dishes were done and the table was set for lunch.

Twice during the interval, as I worked, Melinda cried out and Debbie jumped up to respond like a rookie fireman at the sound of an alarm. Each time, she attempted to feed the baby but had no success.

"Should we try a bottle?" I asked anxiously after the second futile attempt. "You know, it doesn't take much to get an infant dangerously dehydrated, Debbie. It's after twelve already."

"Of course I know." Debbie sank back on the sofa. "When I was in training, we used to have to feed some of the babies intravenously. But I'll wait it out. When she gets hungry, she'll eat."

That, obviously, was that.

I went back to the kitchen and took my frustration out on the dirty floor until Tim and Pete came back with groceries and such.

"Did the baby drink anything yet, honey?" Pete asked Debbie, as the four of us finally sat down for a quick soup and sandwich.

"She will." Debbie looked at me as she answered.

85

"There's nothing to worry about."

While were eating, Melinda cried out for the umteenth time.

"Why don't you just finish your sandwich?' I asked Debbie, as she jumped to attention again. "It won't hurt her to cry for a few minutes, Debbie. It might even give her an appetite."

Debbie looked horrified.

"I would never let my baby cry," she declared vehemently. "It's psychologically bad for a child. Really, Mother," she finished, on her way out of the room, with Pete beside her, "how could you even suggest anything like that?"

The moment we were alone, Tim started to laugh.

"What's funny?" I grumbled over the edge of my teacup.

"You," he promptly replied. "You should have known Debbie would never go for that emancipated motherhood approach which you chose. And if you remember, most women didn't."

As Tim spoke, it all came back to me. How adamantly I had rebelled when Debbie was born against the very theories which Debbie was now espousing! Even then, the Gospel on child care taught that heroic, unmitigated service on a mother's part was a guarantee of freedom from all psychological ills for the offspring. The concept is predicated upon two noteworthy premises: First, that every time a baby cries he has good reason for so doing (a supposition which rates infants higher mentally than most adults I know); and second, that good parents, despite obvious communication barriers, should therefore hasten to satisfy those wants (the line of reasoning here assuming that a baby's wants, unlike those of other human beings, are always attainable, always good for him, and always nobly disinclined to take advantage of the provider).

Accordingly, I had decided early on that Debbie would be allowed to cry it out if she were dry and fed. The subsequent training period that both Tim and I had endured—the incredible iron willpower it had taken to let her howl was something only the early Christians facing the lions in the Roman Arena could have matched. The sound of crying had haunted us for at least two terrible weeks. Like the wail of a never-ending siren in our ears, that nauseating, continuous, disheartening sound of infant crying was following us through walls, through doors, above the stereo. It had echoed in our minds even when we were out of reach on a night off in a distant restaurant. It had been inescapable.

There had been critical moments when we nearly succumbed and almost rushed in to pick her up—only to stop just in time, as we reminded each other that the sole point in picking a baby up when it cries is for the simple parental joy of shutting it up. There had been critical moments when we discussed understandingly and without surprise a newspaper account of a man who had injured his child in an attempt to silence it—assuring ourselves all the while that only a weak character could have become so unnerved.

Eventually, of course, the moment of victory came. Debbie made her adjustment to peaceful co-existence and I could relinquish my hold on the Cradle That Rocks The World.

Tim obviously could see from the expression on my face that it was all coming back to me. "And do you remember," he went on, as if I had spoken aloud, "the God-awful flack we got from everyone around us?"

The memory made us both laugh.

Tim's mother had protested frantically: "Something must be the matter with Debbie. Babies always cry for a reason!"

"Not at all," we had insisted. "Babies can't talk. They cry instead—and they don't need a reason."

Tim's father had worried also, "It seems inhuman. Won't she choke or something? Maybe there's a pin sticking her. Shouldn't you go and see?"

By the end of one week, Debbie's crying was too much for anyone but Tim and me to bear. Tim's parents no longer came to our house because of the racket, and my mother hung up the receiver if she heard the baby's crying over the telephone.

"Weren't we persistent?" I marvelled, living it over again in a quick flashback.

"Just like Debbie about her position on babying." Tim said it so quietly, yet firmly, that it almost went over my head.

"Oh." The full weight of Tim's remark hit me suddenly. "I see what you're saying? that Debbie, like me, would no more surrender one iota of her freedom of action than Washington would at Valley Forge."

"Exactly." Tim was pleased with my response. Then he asked me pointedly, "And how do you think our folks felt about all of our shenanigans?"

"The way I feel right now." It was a strange realization for me. "But there was one difference, sweetie. They could say their piece and we didn't bite their heads off. They could make all the grumbling noises they liked—you know, the way the Grandfather comes through on the deep bass in *Peter and the Wolf*."

Tim smiled at the analogy. "That is a difference," he conceded.

"A major one," I interrupted. "They didn't have to bottle it up—even if we didn't listen or do as they said."

"But the result was pretty much the same, you know." Tim paused for a moment and then added, even more seriously, "What bothers me most about the silence is having to stand by with a grown child and be unable to speak out and keep him or her from making some of the same mistakes we made when we were young. Sure, everyone makes mistakes in life, but it all somehow seems wasted if our children can't learn something from ours and go on, at least, to make a different batch of their own."

"It doesn't make sense, does it?" I agreed sadly. "But that's the way it is. And that's what I have to remember when I listen to Debbie."

"You're doing fine." Tim assured me, reaching over for my hand.

"I'm trying," I answered, grateful for the recognition. "You know, honey, Debbie doesn't even know what's going on with you and me. I'm beginning to feel schizophrenic. Every time Debbie comes up with one of her gems of wisdom, I think of a reply inside me and say nothing or something else to her."

"Save it all for me," Tim wasn't joking. "I'll listen. I'll understand even if I won't always agree. How's that?"

It was a pact—more solemn than most of the agreements entered into by any world powers. And eventually it became our way of grandparent life.

Even that first day, that brief, private talk in the kitchen was a comfort, and helped me to hold to the necessary perspective until we left. When, for example, Debbie held out for three more tries at feeding Melinda and didn't succeed until two o'clock, I said nothing at all. When similarly, she kept popping up like a Jack-in-the-Box every time Melinda made a sound, I looked meaningfully at Tim but held my peace. When, excruciatingly, she reacted to every minimal feel of dampness in the baby's diaper as if it were an unprovoked act of aggression and seemed prepared to spend the rest of her maternal life catching it as it came, I remained as impassive and unresponsive as a ventriloquist's dummy.

Fortunately, there were diversions throughout the long, hot afternoon as a stream of visitors made their pilgrimage to pay their respects to the new baby and the new mother. Excellent diversions, I would say, because they brought with them my next lesson in grandparenthood. The censorship imposed by the generation gap is graciously lifted whenever the older generation's viewpoint supports the opinion of the younger generation. In fact, in those comparatively rare instances, such participation in a discussion is most welcome and a grandparent suddenly becomes what he always used to be in the olden days: A venerated seer.

89

The first arrival was Pete's mother and father who came in complaining loudly about their unexpected detour from the hospital to the apartment. Had anything happened? Was Debbie alright? Did it have something to do with the baby?

It was amusing to me to note the abrupt silence that came over both of them as Debbie very nonchalantly repeated the assurance she had given Tim and me before, "I just got fed up with the hospital routine and decided to come home." I could almost supply the expurgated dialogue that I could see passing beteween them as Mr. Driscoll raised his eyebrows and Mrs. Driscoll shrugged her shoulders—almost imperceptibly—in reply.

Mrs. Driscoll rallied first. "Well, we are going to get a good look at that baby, aren't we?" She asked, leading her husband towards Melinda's room. "No, no dear," she exclaimed as Debbie started to get up. "Don't you disturb yourself any more than necessary. You know, my father was a doctor and he always said too much activity too soon after a delivery led to women's troubles in middle age. You just take it easy."

Mr. and Mrs. Driscoll disappeared down the hallway. As we sat in silence in the living room, we could hear her greet the baby with an easy flow of what is commonly known as "baby talk", "And how is our itsy bitsy babykins today?" She spoke in that high-pitched falsetto that so many people use in addressing children, and Debbie, listening, grimaced.

"I detest 'Baby talk,' " she said flatly. "No one is going to teach my child to speak any retarded version of pig-latin."

"Eureka!" I thought, "for once we agree."

Aloud, I said, "Relax, honey. I know how you feel, but isn't it nice that Melinda is only not quite two days old, so that her powers of hearing are not fully developed and her ability to understand is nil?"

Debbie smiled appreciately and I grinned back.

Then we heard Mr. Driscoll clear his throat and ask his

wife, "Sweetie-pie, whom do you think this young one looks like?"

There was a long silence while the question was being carefully pondered.

"More like Pete," Mrs. Driscoll finally said. "Don't you think so, honey?"

"Definitely." He didn't hesitate. "She has the Driscoll chin."

"You're absolutely right." Mrs. Driscoll sounded relieved and pleased. "They say it's good luck for the first-born, if it's a girl, to resemble the father."

"Just take a look," Mr. Driscoll continued his anatomical analysis piece by piece. "Wouldn't you say that her mouth is Peter's all over again? And the nose? And didn't you tell me yesterday that her eyes are blue?"

In the living room, Debbie and Pete and Tim and I struggled to control our laughter.

"I could have told you this was coming," I told the three of them. "Families always dissect a newborn just like that. It's sort of like staking a claim."

Just then the doorbell rang again and Pete ushered in his Aunt Dorothy.

"My God, Debbie," she boomed as she entered. "I had a devil of a time catching up with you two. Skipped out on us, didn't you?" Aunt Dorothy was the outdoor type—a female equivalent of the Marlboro ads. She dropped her knapsack (that kind of handbag) on a chair and continued her comments as she, too, headed for Melinda's crib. "I tell you, girl, you look damn pale. Hope you're not too disappointed because you didn't come up with a boy. You know what they say, Better luck next time!"

She exited on this happy note, which raised protesting hair on my head and callouses on my palms as I gripped them. To see the ancient Battle of the Sexes carried in this way even unto the womb in these supposedly emancipated days was extremely discouraging. The truth is that this premium on boys had always puzzled and infuriated me.

91

On a purely factual basis—excluding the hunt for a husband at which statistics prove women are adequately skilled anyway, and the dubious perpetuation of the familial cognomen ("What's in a name?")—the modern female generally lives longer than the male; maintains closer relationships usually with her parents; rules the American roost, if by indirection only; and by virtue of her sex, still receives many of the privileges, immunities and courtesies (outside of a subway seat) thereunto belonging.

So engrossed was I in my own reaction to Pete's Aunt Dorothy, that I didn't notice Debbie was getting ready to take off in the same direction. "All Pete and I ever wanted was a normal, healthy child," she fumed. "This antiquated emphasis on boy babies is nuts. And I resent it!"

"Resent what?" Mr. and Mrs. Driscoll had come into the living room while Debbie was speaking and were obviously uneasy that they might have somehow offended.

"Oh, it's just Aunt Dot again," Pete hastily explained. "She made one of those cracks about Melinda being kind of second-best because she's a girl."

"Oh, I'm sure Dorothy didn't mean anything really by that remark," Mrs. Driscoll said, defending her sister. "Lots of people talk that way."

"Well, they shouldn't!" Debbie was still angry. "Maybe it used to be a man's world way back, but women aren't second class citizens anymore—not in these days!"

"And as for sex in relation to babies," I chimed in, equally roused, "I've never been able to understand how it's anything more significant than a question of pink or blue. If you ask me, the average baby is as sexless as an amoeba anyway. Remember those two children in *The Decameron* who couldn't tell whether a nude painting was that of a boy or a girl because the subject had no clothes on? Well, I can never label a baby accurately unless it has its diaper off."

There was an easing of tension in the laughter that followed, and Debbie and I laughed, too. She looked at me fondly, appreciatively, and I gloried in the glow: The humble subject had found favor—temporarily—in her majesty's sight. What a crazy, terrible inequality there is between the generations!

Then Debbie made a last, noteworthy observation. "I guess it's all a matter of point of view," she said. "And as far as I'm concerned, the only difference I find between girl and boy children is purely anatomical; and the only distinction resulting from this difference is the remarkable ability of boys to urinate standing up and over their heads."

Aunt Dorothy's reentrance during Debbie's summation had gone unnoticed. She smiled with the rest of us at the end of it, although she was plainly wounded and as plainly determined to bear it as well as the Boy on the Burning Deck.

Fortunately, the doorbell rang again and then again and then again, each time bringing more relatives who seemed bent on holding an impromptu Old Home Week over poor Melinda.

"Just look," one visitor could be heard to exclaim, "that baby is laying on a cotton pad right over the rubber pad. Doesn't Debbie have a decent sheet?"

"Did you notice they're using cornstarch instead of talcum powder?" someone else pointed out. "I thought Pete had a job now in his father's office."

Debbie sat on the living room sofa looking pale and more wretched each time a newcomer arrived.

"How can we stop them?" she finally, tearfully asked Tim and me. "It isn't even right to have that mob in there with a newborn. What can I do to get them out?"

For Tim, it was plainly his little girl needing help again. Without a moment's delay, he tore into the bedroom like an angry bull at a red flag. We couldn't hear exactly what he said but it had something to do with the germ theory of disease; and in just a few minutes, the relatives left the apartment in a mass exodus like cattle stampeding through an open field.

"Now we're going also," Tim told Debbie and Pete when the door had closed behind the last visitor. "You've had a long and a hard day. For heaven's sake, Debbie, get some rest. You'd never have had to wear yourself out this way if you'd stayed in the hospital. They limit the people who can come in and they look after the baby and they bring you your meals. Did you think managing a house and a new-born would be a game? Don't you know it's a full-time job?"

It was the closest to honesty either of us had come in months in our relationship with Debbie—but it was the wrong time for bluntness or candor. She was obviously too exhausted and too upset for any such encounter now—especially with us. Besides which, there was also the perennial realization that Tim himself, when he calmed down, would be the first to admit: It was really no use to say much of anything anyway: grown children are as impervious to parental advice as is the Rock of Gibraltar.

Wearily, I stood up and made ready to leave. On a sudden impulse—with my purse and sweater on my arm and even after I had kissed Debbie goodby—I took Tim's hand and walked with him back into Melinda's room for a farewell look.

Truly it has been said, "Heaven lies about us in our infancy." As we stood there, close together, watching the sleeping infant and listening to the quiet, even breathing of that tiny, perfect form, a beautiful, unearthly kind of fulfillment stirred my heart. Dimly, almost instinctively, and without any real understanding of what is meant or would mean, I could sense the bond that linked this child and us.

"Debbie's baby!" I whispered wonderingly to Tim in much the way they must have told the news at Bethlehem.

"Our grandchild," he whispered back, squeezing my hand.

And for the first time in all that hectic, frustrating, turbulent, first grandparent day—in spite of all the barriers that endlessly seemed to keep bogging us down—the idea sounded not only possible, but fine.

Chapter VI

FOR WHOM THE BELL TOLLS

GRANDPARENTHOOD is actually as much a complex state of being as adolescence or middle age. To most people, however, it is something as fixed and obvious and beyond transactional analysis as the State of Liberty. The way it is usually told: A grandparent *is* and a grandparent *does;* but nobody really stops to think how and what a grandparent feels.

In reality, it is the internal adjustments to even the fact of grandparenthood that are some of the most difficult to make. You are moving along in your own life, blissfully unaware of the passage of time, and purposefully piloting your own course as if all of this would go on forever. Then, lo and behold, a grandchild is born.

Suddenly, you become a member psychologically of another generation—the older generation. No longer do you rate topbilling in the family soap opera which had seemed, only the day before, to be as inexhaustible as a new box of Kleenex, in which each phase played out sent a new one popping up. No longer are you a principal actor in the script—and often you have no lines.

All of this I could sense almost from the day of Melinda's homecoming, but the full weight of complete realization took a while longer. Little by little—with the inevitability and insidiousness of a man growing a beard—I found myself struggling to cope with many of these personal and private emotional adjustments that all new grandparents, sooner or later, must make. And I began, specifically, in a kind of instinctive reaction to my repeated encounters with one of the most exasperating and slanderous presumptions that any civilization has ever perpetrated against any segment of its population: the incredible belief that old age and senility—in varying degrees—are indigenous to grandparenthood.

In the very beginning, it was mainly just a joke between Tim and me.

"Hi, Grandma," he would love to tease in the weeks following Melinda's birth. "Don't you think you're showing too much leg in that mini-skirt, for your age and station in life?"

"Hi, Grandpa," I would tease right back. "Better not hug me so hard. Remember your arthritis."

Funny. Funny. Funny.

Then, as more time passed and more people heard that Tim and I had become grandparents, we began to hear many serious variations on this theme which could not be laughed off.

"Don't tell me you're a grandmother!" This was one favorite refrain as I got looked over the way a microbe hunter peers at a slide under his microscope. "I must say it doesn't show."

"Well, who would have believed it?" was another common response, accompanied by the same kind of intense scrutiny. "You certainly don't look like it."

"Really, Edwina"—and this was the blockbuster from a long-time friend—"I never realized you were that old."

The implications were much clearer than the writing on Belshazzar's wall, and I didn't need to be a Daniel to interpret what was being said. Because I was a grandmother, I was, all at once, old. The kindest comment that could be offered, therefore, was that my decrepitude was not readily apparent—as if I had somehow been preserved in formaldehyde at a more tender age. Remarkable, wasn't it!

So consistent and unrelenting was this kind of propaganda, moreover, that it seemed impossible to protest and proclaim that I was only in my late forties. Who believes any woman's version of her personal statistics anyway? In addition to which I discovered my own self so much affected by the whole concept that I began to feel—even though I knew better—that some strange and disturbing conversion must have taken place when I wasn't looking: with the end result that I had become sixty-seven instead of forty-seven overnight.

I can still remember staring carefully into my bathroom mirror on several occasions and wondering silently, "Am I really old but not facing it?"

As far as I had ever been able to tell, neither Tim nor I had ever had any aversion to growing old as such. On the contrary, we had always greeted each birthday as if it were manna from Heaven—both of us properly and gratefully aware that another notchmark had been made in our belts by the grace of God, and that the only alternative to the aging process was deadly.

Not, either, that we were at all anxious to speed up the process. For my money, the man who said life begins at forty, while voicing an undeniably encouraging sentiment, was still only making the best of a bad bargain!

But I also was uncomfortably aware that one of the greatest weaknesses in human nature is man's instinctive refusal to see what he does not wish to see. Inevitably, there is an unexplainable, intractable blindness that often overwhelms the most alert and astute of us when we are brought face to face with unpleasant reality—a kind of *"might blindness,"* you might call it, since it is a wilful and not a physical defect. Even when the earth shakes beneath our feet and the clouds crash and the boulders loom perilously close above our heads, we are likely to protest, "Impossible! It just can't be!" Even when the piles of disagreeable evidence are forged like iron chains around our shrinking

97

necks, the stubborn cry is still humanly heard, "Maybe so—but I don't believe it!"

What's more, there is a strength and a persistence in self-delusion that stems directly from the fact that while it is admittedly a dangerous weakness at times, it is also always a wonderful thing. It is the source of hope that springs eternal in the human breast, the core of everyday fortitude to endure what can't be cured—the most effective antidote in many cases for poisonous despair. With it, each day can have the courage and comfort of a Walter Mitty pipedream; without it, life has a tendency to close down on us with all the bludgeoning, butchering force of a cheap mouse trap.

"Tell me the truth, sweetie," I confronted Tim finally with the whole bit one day, "are we really in the 'old' category? I know I don't think that you are or that I am—but is it just that I haven't been facing reality?"

I knew I could count on Tim for stark honesty. He had never been one of that vast school of husbands who pride themselves on the fact that they always try to keep bad news from their "dear little women." Fortunately, we had both never been able to see the value of my inevitably finding out on Thursday what happened on Tuesday, especially when the bad news thus concealed concerned major events like war, pestilence and death. I had taken this stand almost from the day we were married, even though I was well aware that there were many adherents to the opposite philosophy who liked to think they could effectively hide from a lady that fact that a brick just fell on her head. In fact, what had probably set me off in my own direction originally had been the prevalence of the secrecy approach in my own background. I will never forget the time my Uncle Henry was so pleased with his maneuvering (a full twenty-four-hour-a-day job, with everyone else whispering excitedly and furtively around and about the victim of his charity) because it took his wife three whole days before she discovered the passing of a dear but distant relative who was due at the end of the week for dinner. "Henry is so considerate," was the unanimous family verdict of approval.

Not so Tim—thank God.

"Honey," he said without one moment's hesitation, "we're definitely not old. Definitely. We're not young either. We're just middle-aged—whatever that means. And the fact is that when I look at you, I see the same 'you' that I married. I'm sure there must be some changes, but believe me, I can't see them."

"That's exactly how I feel," I exclaimed. "But they keep cramming this 'old' stuff down my throat until I began to feel I must be indecent to be appearing in public without my cane or walker. Do you know what I mean?"

"I know." Tim sat down beside me and held my hand. "I get it, too," he reminded me, "especially from the young lawyers in the office. In a way, though, it's always been around, honey. Each generation kind of pushes the one ahead of it as much off the center of the stage as possible."

"And as soon as possible," I agreed. "Remember how Debbie used to categorize everything that I told her about my growing up—even when she was a very little girl—as something that took place long, long ago 'in the olden days?' "

We both laughed at the memory.

"And it always irked you even while it amused you," Tim recalled, "because she obviously thought of those 'olden days' the way you and I think of prehistoric times—something as far back as the dinosaurs."

"Well, this premature senility imposed on grandparents irks me a lot more," I declared. "I'm far enough along the pike and I don't like the feel of being thought older."

Like it or not, though, there wasn't anything I could do about it except to turn the other cheek—and not in any Christian spirit, either. Nor was Tim's assurance that we were definitely not old of much lasting comfort. For the first time in my life, I looked at middle age squarely in the face and that in itself was a heroic adjustment. What's more, the whole grandparent routine forced me to look at it again and again and again.

One such encounter, for example, was the direct result of our attempt to fix up the spare room as a place for Melinda to stay when Debbie and Pete would come for a visit. It was my friend, Hilda Davis, who alerted me to this aspect of grandparenting.

"You're going to need a crib and a high chair, at least," she advised me over the phone one day.

"What for?" I asked naively.

"For Melinda," she replied. "Where are you going to put her when they come by?"

"Oh." I had never thought of that before.

"Don't you have some old equipment left over from Debbie's babyhood?" Hilda continued briskly.

"I think so." I really wasn't sure.

"Well, go dig it all up, clean it and get it into usable shape," was her final suggestion. "A lot of the girls rent things when their grandchildren come, but that adds up to a lot of money over a period of time. Check it out, Edwina, and see how you're fixed."

So I checked it out one rainy, Saturday afternoon with Tim's help—if you could call it help. Tim's natural, male aversion to any form of housekeeping always made his cooperation on all domestic projects a strange mixture of chivalry and involuntary servitude.

"Are you sure this is necessary?" he asked, as he followed me with undisguised reluctance to the spare room.

"Yup," I answered, ignoring his customary unwillingness the way one ignores the familiar squeaking of an old screen door. "Come on, sweetie. This is a perfect day for this kind of thing. It's so wet outside that we might as well do something worthwhile inside. I'm sure glad that Hilda reminded me about this. After all, Melinda's six weeks old already so we should get prepared right away."

I emphasize the "preparation" angle since Tim and I always liked to jest about our usual lack of foresight in many

100

of the areas that crop up in everyday life. Traditionally, while the rest of the American population buys summer clothes in the winter and winter clothes in the fall, Tim and I were inveterate umbrella-in-the-rain and first-hot-day-for-a-bathing-suit purchasers.

"O.K., O.K.," Tim laughed. "Where do we start?"

We were in the spare room by then and it was a mess. There were enough stacks of rubbish to fill a Salvation Army truck: broken, dilapidated dolls from Debbie's "olden days," two lopsided chairs, half-torn Valentine cards, outdated theatre programs and three packing boxes as replete with family relics as an Egyptian tomb.

"Let's shove this stuff to one side for now," I decided, "and try to set up the crib. Do you know where it is? We did keep it, didn't we, Tim?"

"We did," he affirmed. "And I think we stood it in pieces, all apart, in the back hall closet."

He was right, so the first thing that went up was the crib—and it was a great disappointment. It was battered and bruised and almost scraped bare in spots on the railing by the little teeth that had bitten there.

"Looks terribly rundown," Tim said, staring at it.

"It sure does," I admitted, "but it will have to do. Maybe I can paint it and decorate it later on."

"Maybe," he answered. "But look at the mattress—the innersprings are broken."

"Only a few," I replied. "It got that way from Debbie's jumping up and down on it. Remember?" Tim nodded and I went on: "It never bothered **Debbie** and it won't Melinda either. Don't you agree?"

"You mean Melinda won't have any basis for comparison." It was not a question that Tim posed. It was a statement of fact.

"It isn't as if she would be living here, sweetie," I said in defense of my point of view. "Just visiting. Besides, there's nothing wrong with a tough mattress anyway. Some people sleep on boards! You know that."

"But not on rocks," he countered, pushing down an offending innerspring that was outer. "Well, if you really think it's all right . . ."

"I do," I interrupted.

"Then I'll go down to the basement and carry the high-chair upstairs." He was out of the room by the time he finished the sentence.

The highchair was even worse than the crib. The poor thing looked like something from a haunted house. It was a caricature of senility—as wheezy and arthritic-ridden as an old man. The stuffing was coming through the seams of the back padding, the safety strap was completely missing, and the footrest, suspended in space by one screw, hung treacherously in mid-air. That it held together at all was a minor miracle; that it was not reposing publicly in the Smithsonian Institute where it so obviously belonged, was our private misfortune.

I stood and stared at both the crib and the highchair in what was almost disbelief. How could they have fallen apart in just so short a time? Wasn't it just yesterday that Debbie was standing there behind those rails, her little hands clenched tightly on the top bar for support? Wasn't that hole in the highchair the very spot where she had dug her toy soldier in and then howled and howled, all red in the face, because she couldn't get it dislodged?

I was so engrossed in my thoughts that I never even noticed Tim reach in to one of the packing boxes and come up with a dusty package that he opened and then held out for my inspection also.

"Look here, honey," he said. "Debbie's first pair of shoes. I can still remember when we got these for her. Can you?"

How could I forget? Buying anything in those early days had been a major and often catastrophic event. We were new at marriage, new at parenthood, and just poor enough for it to be more inspiring than intimidating. Debbie had had no separate nursery of her own, but had been installed

102

in a corner of our bedroom which was cleared for her by pushing the dresser out of the way. Her first pair of shoes, consequently, like everything else at the time, had been celebrated as noisily, if not as lavishly, as a bang-up Fourth of July.

"Oh, Tim!" I could hardly speak. "It makes me feel so old—as if it all happened a thousand years ago."

"Or yesterday." Tim replaced the shoes, then came over and held me close. "They grow up when you're not even watching. They sort of sneak up on you in little baby steps you never notice until they've suddenly covered a giant's stride. One day they're infants and the next day they're grown people. It doesn't take a thousand years. It's just that the parents are always the last to know."

"Well, I know," I said wistfully, "and it still makes me feel sort of sad—sort of old."

The feeling kept being reinforced in many other ways directly or indirectly associated with the advent of Melinda—and the most painful of these came from our dear daughter herself. As the months of her motherhood progressed, so did Debbie's arpartheid practices in regard to our two generations. Whatever had been espoused by Tim and me as parents was disowned by her; if we had done and said it, she didn't and wouldn't.

It soon became unmistakably clear that in the realm of living philosophies, Debbie and I were and would forever be two parallel lines that follow in the same direction but never meet. And I couldn't help wishing that God would be a little more consistent and considerate when it comes to this irrational business of matching children to parents—if only for the continued domestic tranquility of the whole tribe.

Of course, none of this was anything as simple or overt as a formal declaration of independence, much less war. No sir! We visited back and forth, we talked on the phone, and we observed all the niceties of our family relationship. It was just that there was such total rejection of everything

103

our parenthood had stood for that inevitably the rejection seemed to extend to us.

Talk about feeling old? Outmoded is exactly that in its most debilitating and crucial form.

For example: Tim and I had never had the kind of allegiance to the Germ theory of Disease that in other fields of history had sent the French marching on the Bastille. We had never attempted to maintain operating room sterility around Debbie as a child, or gone to some of the fanatical lengths that flourished in that day. The middle course had been our avowed goal and we liked to think we had found it.

Imagine then—if you can—our state of shock when we had to stand by in silence and watch Debbie establish the kind of sanitation for Melinda that would have been banned by the authorities—even in the Casbah. Pacifiers were picked off the dirty floor and stuffed in the baby's mouth; spoons and cups were eaten from in common by Debbie and Melinda; dropped foods were retrieved and fed to the child; bottles were casually rinsed but not washed thoroughly.

"Don't look so surprised," Debbie would say to our startled faces. "People don't go to extremes anymore about things like these. Do you realize that your generation was as afraid of germs as the generation before yours was scared of the bogyman?"

Most of Debbie's commentaries were as dogmatic and undiplomatic as that—and always consistently inconsistent with what she remembered or misremembered from her own childhood.

"You know, Mother," she told me one day, "I'm not going to beat Melinda the way you used to beat me."

"Beat you?" Fortunately, Tim was present at this session and could cover me while I recovered from the false charge. "Debbie," he said, "your Mother and I used physical force on you exactly one time in your life—and you sure deserved it. Don't you remember how it was?"

Reluctantly, Debbie remembered. "Well," she said, after a pause, "maybe you didn't exactly hit me, but you yelled a lot. I'm not going to be like that with my daughter."

Debbie was fairly new at motherhood then and she obviously classified Melinda as Celestial Material. Her voice went three octaves higher whenever she spoke to the child. It was ridiculously apparent that she thought Melinda's presence in her home should have automatically converted the place into a national shrine. Naturally, by the time Melinda was over two and had advanced to writing on the walls, telling lies and say "No" to everything, Debbie's sweet falsetto gradually gave way to the Call of the Wild. There were times, in fact, when the tone of voice she directed at her disobedient pride and joy was cold enough to deep-freeze a side of beef!

Still, there was no use in saying anything then—and there never has been to this day. Besides, if I ever really began to rebut each point as it surfaced, where would I ever stop? Name it—and there was a schism between our views that was deeper than the Grand Canyon.

Take the whole question of discipline. I am fully aware that most modern child psychologists in their current canonization of the young would tend to deny even the concept of a "spoiled brat." As far as I had always been concerned, however, the rose by any name very definitely exists. From Debbie's infancy onward, therefore, I had been militantly opposed to the prevalent type of miniature, uninhibited, over-secure, under-civilized kind of youngster so often encountered in polite society nowadays. These creatures I had always deplored as a public menace and a private horror, easily recognizable for what they are and, if possible, to be avoided like a known typhoid carrier.

In restaurants, theatres and other unrestricted areas, I had often watched them disturb the general peace: Breathing down the backs of people's necks over the tops of restaurant booths; running up and down crowded or darkened aisles; spilling food and milk with reckless abandon; and howling, whatever the time or the place, at the slightest whim or at any hint of curtailment of these endearing activities.

In the sanctity of their homes, I had frequently been subjected to their same undaunted pace: Their vomiting astonishingly at the drop of one cross word; climbing mercilessly over the furniture and anyone sitting thereon; whining noisily and sulkily if temporarily deprived of attention; commandeering egotistically any grown-up conversations with innumerable interruptions, as well as pointed suggestions for topics of talk, like: "Mamma—you tell them what I did to the minister on Sunday!"; and shrieking maddeningly if ever balked.

With all of this in mind, Tim and I had worked all through the years to escape from the resultant Downtrodden Parents' Brigade into which most mothers and fathers were conscripted. It had been our combined and firm opinion that another batch of this type of children could easily result in complete race suicide—and we had fought for our emancipation and freedom from parental abuse with the same kind of determination that MacArthur had fought for the Philippines. What's more, we had succeeded—at least to our own satisfaction—in establishing a family regime that was not only livable but utterly devoid of totalitarianism on either side.

Debbie was fed discipline along with her pablum and Similac. Good manners were distilled into her everyday routine. Punishments—after a kind of Supreme Court deliberation on Constitutional issues—were imposed by us judiciously and promptly, but quite creatively. They could range all the way from such things as a ban on television and/or dessert to out-and-out complete house arrest; and never, I might also add, did they ever manifest the least tinge of a Simon Legree let loose with a guillotine.

There were play areas for Debbie and restricted areas in which no play was allowed—both meticulously observed.

"I'm not going to wait for a home of my own until after

106

Debbie grows up," I had announced grimly to Tim one night after her explorations through our living room earlier that day had left a trail of torn books, broken figurines and spotted upholstery in her wake. "We need a place unmarred by baby paraphernalia and destruction in which to relax and we need it now!"

Debbie, therefore, had originally been allowed only strictly supervised excursions to the living room. She had been subjected to careful explanations regarding the fragility and significance of many of the pieces in it. She had been taught to look but not touch; and indeed it had not been too long before she could be safely permitted to roam about on her own, admiring my "objects of art" but never destroying a single one—almost as if she were a visitor in a picture gallery, held back by an invisible velvet rope.

That was Debbie, the child.

Then came Debbie, the Mother.

"I'm not going to inhibit Melinda if I can possibly help it," she told me very seriously one day when she was gathering up the shreds of a Chinese lamp that had just been smashed to smithereens. "You were always warning me not to touch this and not to break that. It was so restrictive!"

"But don't you mind losing your lovely things?" I asked wonderingly. "That lamp was a wedding present from Pete's Great-Aunt Thelma. She told me that it was a farewell gift many years ago from the people when she retired from her missionary work in the Orient."

"Oh, I don't like losing that kind of thing," Debbie conceded. "But this is Melinda's home, too."

"Of course," I answered, "and she has her room and the kitchen and the dining room for wandering around in freely. Don't you want a comfortable place for you and Pete to enjoy also?"

"Honestly, Mother," Debbie closed the discussion abruptly; "I know what you're getting at, but that's not my way. I'll just go out and refurnish when Melinda's grown up enough to cooperate voluntarily. Until then, we'll just grin and bear it."

Unfortunately, every visitor to Debbie's home (including Tim and me) had to grin it and bear it also. It might be a toy car that tripped you as you entered; it might be the pointed edge of a wooden block that pierced your backside when you sat down on the sofa; it might be Melinda herself who plastered you with modelling clay as you sipped your Coke. Whatever the specifics at any given time, it was usually impossible to really relax, because it always seemed absolutely necessary to maintain a suspicious watch for fresh dangers, more or less the way old-timers in tornado country keep a constant, uneasy vigil over each moving cloud and rising wind.

I can still think back to the many times I would reach down, without a word about it, to excise some painful plaything "foreign body" from my person while smiling on politely at Debbie and Pete, and continuing our conversation as if not only didn't my left hand know what my right was doing, but that both hands belonged to somebody else!

It was none of the physical discomfortures, however, that were as difficult to swallow as mountain boulders. It was the vast philosophical differences between Debbie and us on the whole concept of parenthood that were incredibly—albeit silently—disturbing. Not only was Melinda comparatively undisciplined, but she was being directed by Debbie from infancy onward on a futile search for a non-existent Fountain of Happiness that Tim and I had long ago decided could only lead to disillusionment and disaster for any child—especially ours.

Not that Debbie's approach was at all unique!

More than ever, in our present civilization, man does *not* live by bread alone. He demands cake (with whipped cream on top) and meat (the choicest cuts) and fresh fruits and vegetables (in variety as well as abundance) and new cars and fur coats and European vacations among Lord knows what else! Accordingly, whether he can afford it or not, it

108

has become man's personal goal in life and the avowed purpose of modern parenthood to give his children "everything," especially the things *he* "didn't have"—be it music lessons and dancing lessons and riding lessons and beautiful clothes and social standing and a B.A. degree, and as much of the general jackpot as his years of struggle and drudgery can buy. In short, it has become fashionable indeed to raise children who must inevitably grow up and face (dangerously untrained) the dull, menial chores and tight, uncomfortable budgets that with very few exceptions are the beginnings, and often the ends, of all our adult lives, as if they were heirs-apparent to a Rockefeller fortune.

Years of observation of this parental rat-race had convinced Tim and me that the only ones who profited from the whole shebang were the psychiatrists and child psychologists who, at the rate of twenty-five to fifty dollars an hour, were ever willing to explain and doctor our increasingly muddled, miserable, self-confessed neurotic population. That our own daughter, therefore, was a member of the opposition aroused enough private talk between Tim and me to fill the Congressional Record.

I say "private talk" with full malice of forethought. We had long ago gone underground as far as open, frank discussions with Debbie could go—and that self-imposed strict censorship was difficult enough to maintain. What made it excruciating to maintain was the fact that as Debbie's personal sense of assurance and importance and accomplishment flourished in the glow of her motherhood, so did her freedom to speak out in every way. With the result that not only did she expound freely and fully on her divergent parental doctrine with all the fervor of a card-carrying Communist parroting the party line, but she began as well to tell us what we should do and why. It was a weird reversal of roles!

"You know, Mother," she would say, never for a moment stopping to think that we had not solicited her opinion, "you and Daddy are so sedentary. Why don't you join some

109

athletic club and start getting more exercise? It's really very important at your age."

Her gratuitous advice included every aspect of our adult lives from proposed vacations ("Really, Daddy, three countries in two weeks is much too strenuous for you and Mother!") to my clothes ("It's all right, I guess, Mother, but isn't it a little too much on the teeny-bopper side—for you?").

"Now, honey," Tim consoled me one day, in an attempt to calm me down after another one of these forays by Debbie, "why should any of her remarks surprise or disturb you? It's just an exaggeration of what's been coming on for years. You know what I mean: The grown-up child syndrome."

Was it?

I stopped for a moment to think it through.

Undeniably, the metamorphosis of children into people can be sheer agony even while it is also one of the most inspiring spectacles in life. On the one hand, it is the true miracle of creation made manifest and comprehensible to all of us. It is the moving revelation of God's infinite splendor—the shining proof in everyday experience of His power and His glory forever.

On the other hand: There is no limit to the areas of heartbreak and treachery that can be cultivated by the more mature child in his responses to his parents. Even as they beam with blind paternal pride at the grown body ("Imagine it! And just yesterday a baby!") and the wonderful mind ("Isn't that really brilliant?"), the doubt and the dread begin.

You talk—he looks bored.

You comment—he disagrees.

You rant—he acts superior.

You insist—and he obliges, but with an infuriating kind of amused tolerance, as if to say, "They *are* parents. Might as well humor the creatures."

Eventually, inevitably, there is an absolute destruction of

parental security. Home becomes a house filled with children who may be familiar-looking strangers: a self-created Fifth Column that can easily overcome and take over a mere mother and father. Flesh of our flesh, blood of our blood though they be, they are suddenly wholly separate and specific entities apart from us. No longer do they automatically echo our views, espouse our causes, or esteem what we esteem because we do. Loyal they may remain, but it is often a token loyalty or one with inner reservations; and the closest filial relationships cannot wipe out those enduring areas of withdrawal, those secret places within the mind and soul that defy parental penetration.

More than this—once the judging has begun, it does not confine itself to the outside world. Gradually, too, parents come under the scrutiny until they stand dangerously, uncomfortably unveiled as mere people, measured and tested by standards of a new generation's making. And the consequences of this whole process are usually as disruptive as they are far-reaching!

Having endured much of this with Debbie, I could not deny Tim's basic contention that what we were witnessing now was an intensification of what he so aptly had labelled "the grown-up child syndrome."

"But it's a lot more than just that," I finally decided when I had completed my quick review of the situation. "The problem is that even Debbie thinks of us as an older generation because we're grandparents now. She's not clear about it by any means, but it's all mixed up inside her with senility and age. She and Melinda are the present and the future; you and I represent the past. Why sweetie, you'll never believe what she told me yesterday!"

"I'll believe anything," Tim assured me laughingly. "What did she say?"

"That you and I didn't need this house anymore because we're just two of us rattling around in it by ourselves. She thought it would make more sense if we just sold the place and settled down in some nice apartment, where we

111

wouldn't have steps to climb or outdoor chores to take care of. How's that?" I unfurled this latest tidbit as triumphantly as a magician pulls a rabbit out of his hat. Then I sat back to savor Tim's reaction.

"Well," he said with a big grin, "at least she didn't suggest a nursing home."

"It's no joke," I stormed back.

"I know it isn't," he conceded more seriously. "And what was your answer to her proposal?"

"That we could manage our lives ourselves I guess," I admitted reluctantly, "I did blow my top a little. I said we weren't in our dotage yet, and that just because she was out of the house didn't mean we had no use for it or couldn't enjoy it. I said that we were letting her do her thing, and that she should let us do ours because it's a two-way street."

Tim sighed audibly. "Did she understand what you were getting at?" he asked.

"Not really," I replied. "She just seemed hurt at my rebuff. Said she didn't mean to hurt my feelings and that she loved us very much."

"Which she does." Tim was emphatic. He took both my hands in his and held them tightly. "Don't you see, honey? There are adjustments in this grandparent business that have to be made on both sides of the fence. Yet because we're older, most of the adjusting has to be done by us."

"But it's hard," I protested, "and not fair."

"So what's new?" Tim laughed as he spoke. "Don't fight it, and before long you'll be so used to what this whole stage of our lives is all about that you'll forget to mind it. Because it really is a new and special time!" Tim paused as he searched for the right words. "How can I make you understand what I mean?" he asked. "Look at it this way, dear. There's nothing to struggle with, nothing to fear. Being a grandparent—moving on in parental relationships—is all part of a phenomenon that's as natural and inevitable as the changing of the seasons."

Tim was so much in earnest, so endearing in his concern that I leaned forward and kissed his cheek.

"I know what you're saying." Now it was my turn to grope for the right words. "It's difficult and it takes a while, but it's entirely normal. You just keep going along from month to month and there's never any sharp, demarcation line between one season and the other—only the sudden, wonderful awareness that the change has come when you weren't even looking and Spring is here!"

"No Spring." Tim corrected me teasingly. "It's Fall."

"Fall?" I repeated the word thoughtfully. Then I started to laugh as I realized what he was telling me. "So what!" I reminded him, at last able to take an impulsive, confident leap over all the hitherto seemingly monumental grandparental and parental adjustments in sight. "That can be a beautiful time of year, too!"

Chapter VII

TO BABY-SIT OR NOT TO BABY-SIT:
IS THERE A QUESTION?

IN THE ordinary course of grandparental life, baby-sitting is definitely no question. On the contrary, it is an undisputed fact of the most elemental magnitude: A chimney smokes; a dog barks; a grandparent baby-sits.

In the face of this kind of an almost irrebuttable presumption, therefore, there is little opportunity to consider the issue and arrive at rational conclusions. Preliminary discussions about the availability of a grandparent's services are rarely undertaken. Instead, all the parties involved—including the poor, entrapped babysitters—act so automatically and promptly upon the expectation, that it would take the courage of a Martin Luther nailing his tenets to the church front door for any grandparent to defy the system openly and say No.

This, in any case, is how it was with Tim and me in the beginning. Much as I would love to report our immediate intelligent assessment of the overall situation and our consequent independent stand, honesty compels me to confess that we reacted initially in as cowardly a fashion as most of our peers.

Melinda was only five weeks old when Debbie and Pete deposited her for the first time in our reluctant care.

"Mother," Debbie asked me on the phone a few days

earlier, "is it all right if we bring the baby over to your house for a few days? Pete's driving up to Montreal on business next week and I'm just dying to go with him! I've been so cooped up in this apartment ever since Melinda was born that I just have to get away. I thought we'd drop her off at your place on the way up. O.K.?"

She made it sound so simple, so light, so natural, as if she were merely suggesting something as inconsequential as some help with a heavy package she was carrying. The word "baby-sit" was never mentioned and I was taken completely by surprise.

"But Debbie," I floundered in reply, "what about your breast feeding? How could we manage?"

"Oh, didn't I tell you?" Debbie answered airily. "That didn't really work out. We'll bring her bottles and things. It's only for three days. What do you say?"

What could I say?

"You could have told her that we were planning on going to the shore this weekend," Tim reminded me when I announced at dinner that Melinda was coming in two days. "Did you forget?"

"Not really," I said apologetically. "But I was caught off guard. Look, sweetie, we'll go next weekend. Do you really mind?"

Tim was only partially appeased. "Honey," he said firmly, "I don't want to get caught up in the baby-sitting business for Debbie. We served our time—and I've been enjoying the way things have finally gotten to be."

I had been enjoying it, too.

At long last, Tim and I had emerged on the other side of the parenthood mountain and resumed our basic identity as a couple. After years of enduring the inroads that Debbie had made into our personal lives, we were free again to laugh and talk and love without interruption—and the freedom was a joy.

The fact is that the uninhibited invasion of a set of parents' inalienable right to amorous as well as general pri-

116

vacy is one of the most exasperating aspects of parenthood. Love that makes the world go round and founds dynasties becomes nothing but a secret undercover agent in the average household. Inevitably, children, who are usually credited with being the tie that binds in family life, are also the most solid wedge that can ever come between two romantically inclined married people, whose inspiration is already adequately hindered by endless responsibility and limited opportunity. Kissing in the parlor in one's own home can become more embarrassingly public than pure passion on a bench in Central Park at high noon.

It had always seemed almost impossible in our case to gird our defenses successfully against Debbie's constant eruptions into our most intimate midst. We would lecture her repeatedly, for example, on the strict requirement that she knock on our bedroom door before entering—whatever the time of night or day. What she responded with, alas, was an accommodation by which she knocked and opened the door almost, but not quite, simultaneously so that Tim and I would fly apart as if a live grenade had landed between us. It was an ingenious kind of obedience which met the letter but not the spirit of the law, and it made us sometimes yearn in frustration for the secure isolation of midnight at Potter's Field.

In a similar vein, I could never begin to count the instances Tim and I had paused in the middle of an important moment in our lives to reach warmly for each other—only to be confronted suddenly by one of Debbie's disgusted commentaries, like, "You're holding hands again. Just like the movies. What silly stuff!"

I remember particularly the time when Tim had won an important case and had come home triumphantly to celebrate.

"Honey," he said happily, "this means we can pay off the balance on the mortgage! Isn't that wonderful? It's hard to believe we've really made it!"

It was a beautiful moment for both of us. We had stood

lost in nearness and a flood of reminiscences, thinking back over the long way we had come. Tim and I had started literally from scratch with an elopement marriage when he was still in law school and I was just out of college. Flaunting every blood relative and every principle of common sense and practicality, we had embarked on a tough, tedious path of life which had ultimately paid huge dividends in mirth, madness and matrimony. And while the added struggle did not necessarily flavor the reward as the proverb tells it ("The harder the struggle, the sweeter the reward"), still it had paid its way in the stronger bonds between the two of us—besides never failing us as an interesting topic of conversation.

So absorbed had we been in sentimental recollection that for a brief moment, it was just like it had been in our distant beginnings: The two of us standing close, alone again, looking deeply into each other's eyes and hearts. It had been a long kiss and a wonderful kiss, until a voice nearby had said with obvious curiosity, "Holy cow!" and we jumped apart. There, in the doorway, had appeared nine-year-old Debbie, watching us with clinical interest.

"How can you breathe when you're doing that?" she had asked next, puckering up her face and shutting her eyes in a grotesque imitation of our behavior.

"Through my ears," Tim had answered with annoyed embarrassment, while I had squirmed self-consciously like a flea-infested dog. "Why don't you make more noise when you walk anyway?"

"Because I'm practicing how to stalk animals—like an Indian."

Debbie's explanations had always been simple and unassailable, just as her interruptions had always been unpredictable. That our love and commitment to each other had survived these handicaps had always been a source of amazement to both of us; that our marriage had taken on new meaning and life with Debbie's departure into her own marriage was something that fills me to this day with the

118

same kind of gratitude and awe that everyone must have felt as they watched Lazarus come forth from the tomb. It had been all that I had hoped for, and more than I had dared to expect!

Hearing Tim express his own sense of appreciation at the dinner table now for our new way of life with just the two of us to do for, made me realize in response how far we had already come as a couple since Debbie had moved out.

"Sweetie," I assured him, "it has been wonderful this past year, hasn't it? Just you and me!"

"Like starting all over again," Tim replied. "Which is why I don't want to get us messed up babysitting Melinda. Good God, honey, think of what we went through for years."

"I've thought," I laughed. "The thousands of meals, punctuated with 'Don't huff your food down, Debbie'. . ."

"Or," Tim interjected, "the lessons in etiquette that went on from course to course: 'Get your elbows off the table/this is not a horse's stable!' Does that sound familiar?"

We were both giggling by then.

"I used to hallucinate about sleeping late," I reminded Tim next. "Debbie always got up at dawn, or just about, and she would disturb me. Remember how irritated I would get? I went after her hammer and tongs and insisted that she'd better not wake me in the mornings. . ."

"So," Tim continued for me, "she would come in silently and stand beside the bed as you slept. Pretty soon you'd become conscious of heavy breathing over you, and nearly jump out of your skin as you came suddenly awake."

"And she could never figure out why I got angry and accused her of getting me up," I finished merrily, "since she had obeyed my orders and had never said a word!" I paused for a moment, then came up with another morsel. "And what about all the times we would retreat to the car for private discussions?" I asked. "Remember that?"

"You mean after we found out she wasn't deaf?" Tim was getting more and more hilarious.

Debbie's unresponsiveness to our shouts in her direction at one stage of her childhood had worried us so much that we were making arrangements to have her hearing tested. We didn't, of course, when we gradually became aware that she had no difficulty knowing what we said when Tim and I would take ourselves to our bedroom and whisper secretively with the door shut, while she presumably was in the kitchen downstairs.

"Oh Tim!" The flood of memories was nostalgic, but it also highlighted the present. "It was excruciating at times and it was fun. I don't regret one moment of it. But it makes what we have at this point even more wonderful. You know what I mean? Now we're people again. We can sit and talk on an adult level, come and go as we please and concentrate on each other. . . ."

"Especially on Saturday mornings when we can stay in bed as late as we like." Tim put this piece in quickly. I blushed as he grinned.

Then I continued: "But then we were primarily a set of parents, and that took precedence over everything else that we could or should have been to each other."

"Well, let's go on being people," Tim replied more seriously. "Not a set of grandparents. I know we're stuck this time, but I don't want us to be taken over like an invading army occupying a conquered territory."

"We won't be," I promised. "Anyway, it's just this weekend."

But what a weekend it turned out to be!

Debbie and Pete rushed in on Friday evening bearing Melinda and enough equipment to start a nursery school. Within five minutes, a folding baby carriage was set up in the middle of the living room; some kind of a "baby-tender" seat was plunked down on the velvet sofa; a large carry-all case was unpacked hurriedly so that bibs and undershirts and baby kimonos and booties were strewn about like confetti after a Main Street parade; and cartons of Pampers, a package of diapers, countless bottles of milk, a box of infant

120

cereal and several cans of formula were spread out in the kitchen.

"Just feed her whenever she cries," Debbie briefed me as she flew about. "I've left a tentative kind of schedule as a loose guide on the counter. You really shouldn't have any problems, Mother. She's such a good little girl."

By this time, Debbie and Pete were almost out the front door. "What about the nights?" I called after them. "Does she sleep through?"

"Mostly." Debbie turned to give me a farewell hug. "Thanks loads, Mother," she said happily; "you don't know how much it means to me to get away. Goodby."

In the silence that followed their departure, Tim and I stared at each other for a long, meaningful moment.

"We've been rampaged." Tim spoke first.

"Well," I reminded him, "you know Debbie's place looks like this most of the time. What do you say we put some order back in here? O. K.?"

It was a fine idea, but at this point, Melinda started to cry.

"Should we feed her?" Tim headed for the kitchen, as I went over to the carriage to check on the diaper.

"Warm the bottle in the saucepan," I called out to Tim. "She's sopped, so I'll change her."

From there on, it was as if we were under siege. We fed; we changed; she cried—and we started all over again. Twice during the night she howled, and we found ourselves at two A.M. wrestling with such a diaper mess that it took both of us to clean it up—and even then we had to resort to dumping her in the bathroom sink.

Matters were complicated further by the fact that Tim and I were both incredibly out of practice with the infant K.P. and the night duty routine. Whereas years before I had had a way with a diaper that was almost a kind of sleight of hand maneuver, my touch with Melinda was awkward and unsure.

In addition, Tim and I were uncomfortably conscious that

121

Melinda was somebody else's property. If I had ever stuck my baby accidentally with a pin—and at some time, I must have—there was nobody to answer to but God and myself. With Melinda, however, it was my sacred duty to return her in as good or better condition than that in which she had been delivered. This responsibility painfully augmented my usual neurotic approach to any kind of borrowing, which was so bad in itself that I had once replaced a neighbor's worn-out hedge clippers with a brand new pair, rather than explain that his had given up the ghost on my bushes.

The climax of the weekend came with an unexpected phone call from my friend Hilda, who wanted Tim and me to meet Larry and her for dinner at a midway point between our two places.

"Baby-sitting?" she practically screamed when I explained why we couldn't go. "Edwina, how did you ever get in that sort of a bind?"

"Oh, come on, Hilda," I protested, trying to make it sound like a joke, "this is our very first time."

"Well, make it your last," she advised. "When Jimmy's first baby was born, he and Susie used to drop Junior off whenever they liked. It never occurred to either of them that Harry and I weren't jumping for joy to be so honored."

"So you told them." Knowing Hilda as I did, there was no need to put this statement in the form of a question.

"Exactly," she replied. "And did it shake them up! From their point of view, there couldn't possibly be anything Harry and I could do by ourselves anyway. You know how it is: the only thing anybody over forty needs or takes is Geritol!"

I couldn't help laughing.

"But it's only too true," I told Tim, after I'd hung up on her promise of a rain-check and reported the conversation back to him. "Debbie seems to think we never do anything important, and never care to anyway. So if we're just sitting here vegetating in our decline, why shouldn't she park Melinda with us?"

"Because," said Tim through a big yawn, "I'm too old to take it anymore. After all, they can't expect to have it both ways, can they? If we're in such a state of decline that our time is expendable, we should also be categorized as lacking the physical stamina to cope with a baby. Surely, that's what God must have had in mind when He more or less limited reproduction to the young. Wherefore, honey," Tim finished grandly, "it's up to you to set the record straight for Debbie. In short, tell her what's what, just as Hilda delivered her own Emancipation Proclamation."

Unfortunately, the opportunity to tell Debbie directly just didn't come for quite a while. Primarily, perhaps, because Debbie's way of enlisting our baby-sitting services was never any kind of a specific encounter that would have opened the door for a frank discussion and a real conclusion.

"By the way," Debbie would say casually, in the middle of a protracted telephone visit, "what are you and Daddy doing this Saturday night?"

"We're having a few couples over for dinner," I would reply as casually and without any awareness of what Debbie was concocting.

"That's super!" she would promptly exclaim. "Pete and I were invited over to the Dexters and I couldn't get a sitter. We'll just drop Melinda off at your house on our way. She'll be fed and all ready to sleep. We'll pick her up on our drive home. You won't even know she's there. O.K.? Do you mind?"

How could I say that I did mind? It would have seemed so unreasonable to Debbie. There was no way to make her understand that even if Melinda did sleep all evening in the bedroom upstairs—which was by no means always the case—it was still like having a time bomb ticking away and knowing that it could go off at any moment. What's more, it often did: If our guests talked too loudly or if the stereo hit a full-blast crescendo. Besides, finally, it was absolutely nerve-shattering to be awakened at one or two in the morning out of a deep sleep, when Debbie and Pete would come stealthily up the stairs to reclaim their daughter.

The subtle babysitting requests were sporadic enough to prevent any organized defenses, yet persistent enough to be burdensome. Moreover, by the time Melinda was close to three years of age, the nature of the babysitting became even more disruptive.

"Grandmuzzer." I would be engrossed in my writing when the little pajama-clad figure would materialize in the doorway. "I need a drink."

Down went the pen. Five characters would be left mentally in mid-air while we marched to the kitchen for some water.

"Grandmuzzer." Twenty minutes later, it was again no apparition; it was just Melinda. "I have to make a wee-wee."

Sometimes it was a request for a story; sometimes for a cookie; sometimes for another drink. It was all par for the usual childhood course, and it might even have been somewhat amusing if it were not by the same token so disturbing. What made it frustrating also, though, was Debbie's insistence that no kind of discipline be exercised by us on Melinda—as if we were going to beat her up!

"Just tell me if she misbehaves," Debbie had mandated, "and I'll talk to her about it myself"—a procedure, incidentally, that put us on the level of a teen-age sitter whose only method of keeping order was the impotent threat that she would tell Melinda's mamma what had happened when her mamma came home. Can you imagine being hamstrung like that?

Another technique that Debbie sometimes used in cornering us for babysitting—and it had all the diplomatic touch of a Henry Kissinger—was what Tim came to call "the weekend play."

124

"You know, Mother," she would announce on a Wednesday or a Thursday over the phone, "Pete and I hardly ever get a chance to visit with you and Daddy anymore. How about if we came on Saturday and stayed over to Sunday? We can really talk."

It was such attractive bait that the first few times I got hooked without a moment's hesitation. It was regrettably true that we rarely had any good conversations anymore: either we were expected to gasp with admiration at each sound Melinda made when she and Debbie and Pete were in our presence, or else they made their drop of Melinda at our house for babysitting purposes with more of a rush than an unfriendly mailman when he leaves a package at the door.

The operational pattern for those weekends, moreover, always turned out to be more of the same: Saturdays were dominated by Melinda; Saturday *nights* (after a family dinner) were dedicated to babysitting while Debbie and Pete went off to a movie ("You understand, don't you, Mother: We hardly ever get out alone anymore!"); and Sunday mornings meant more baby-sitting because Debbie and Pete were just dying to have an intimate brunch at the Holiday Inn—or Ciro's—or what have you.

On two occasions that I distinctly remember—and this was climactic—Tim and I, finding ourselves saddled with Melinda when some special social function suddenly came up, hired our own baby-sitters to baby-sit for us so that we could be free to go. A turnabout, incidentally, that bothered us but not our daughter.

"This is insane," Tim exploded the night after such a substitution had been made at our expense for the second time. It isn't the money that I mind; it's the imposition—having to scrounge around for a sitter! What did they have a baby for if they can't accept the responsibility of having to be restricted in their social life because of her? Why do we have to be penalized?"

"Now darling," I said soothingly, "you're absolutely right in saying we shouldn't be penalized. But you're not entirely fair about the responsibility angle."

"What do you mean?" he challenged.

"Well, think back to when Debbie was small," I answered. "Didn't we also yearn for some escape?"

The blessings of family life notwithstanding, there comes a time in every parent's life when the grass on the other side of the playpen looks irresistibly greener. Daily tasks assume an air of unusual monotony. The pleasant patience of yesterday begins to wear dangerously thin.

All at once, you straighten up in the middle of cajoling a spoonful of cereal into a tightly closed mouth and realize that this has been going on for ages and ages—all of weeks, months and maybe even years. The yearning to get away from it all sweeps through your soul like a sudden tornado leaving domestic destruction in its wake.

"Don't you really remember how it was?" I prodded Tim. "You used to say that all the mothers and fathers of the world should form a union of their own and strike immediately for shorter working hours and more time off. I even volunteered to be a charter member, and parade with a six-foot sign proclaiming that parents have rights, too."

Tim smiled reluctantly at the memory. It had been one of our favorite themes: the workers of this nation embrace an eight-hour day and two weeks' vacation as a matter of course; the maids of the households worship before the accepted every Thursday and every other Sunday "out." In fact, the good Lord has decreed a Sabbath day of rest for all of his children, apparently—except parents.

"But we did for ourselves," Tim reminded me. "We got baby-sitters when we could, and when we couldn't, like it or lump it, we stayed at home."

"Correct." Then I added: "Your parents lived in California and mine were equally unavailable. Maybe that was why. Anyway, baby-sitters cost a lot of money these days—when you can get them—and Debbie and Pete don't have much to shell out. Besides, do you remember what we endured with baby-sitters?"

They were often unreliable; they usually consumed all the edibles in the place; they generally inspected every private but unlocked drawer and closet they could find; and although they were conspicuously alone on our return, there was often enough telltale evidence of orgiastic activity left behind to make us uneasy and suspicious of the worst.

"Sure I remember some of those kids took over when we went out," Tim conceded. "But come to think of it, we took Debbie with us most of the time when we went on vacation, didn't we? Why can't she take Melinda?"

"She can," I replied, "but she probably senses already what we found out long ago for ourselves: vacationing with a child is like taking a busman's holiday—not much fun."

And it wasn't.

In the first place, for too many hotel-keepers, children were most unwelcome as guests. The version we encountered of the old "Children should be seen but not heard" was "Children should be neither heard nor seen"—a philosophy that was epitomized in the many advertisements that warned: "No Dogs or Children Allowed."

I can still almost hear Tim's angry declaration in this regard. "That smacks to me of the worst possible type of discrimination. It's bad enough to refuse to accommodate people who appear with children—even if they do it tactfully and pleasantly. But by putting it in high-pressure print in this way, they make me feel as if I were an Untouchable overstepping the bounds whenever I walk into such a place carrying Debbie. Don't they realize anyway that by the time they reach two years of age, most children resemble the human rather than the canine element?"

In any case, there being no alternative kennel in which to park Debbie, we did take our holidays en famille. Although I never much liked it, we became quite skilled at keeping Debbie from literally and figuratively stepping on other people's toes. Equally important, we grew slyly adept at keeping them off ours. When overfriendly strangers urged Debbie to suck on their fingers, or tried to plant wet kisses on her mouth, Tim and I had a vanishing technique worked out that would have baffled the F.B.I. We could not, however, escape the incredibly annoying tendency people have of regarding the presence of a child with its parents as free license for open hunting. Waitresses, fellow guests, transients—one and all would come flocking forth with suggestions, reminiscences and advice for the child-blessed couple. Tim's abrupt departure never stopped them; my pained, fixed smile never discouraged them any more than my lack of comment. It was like having a pack of drones swarm down on me with loud buzzing; and it always inspired the same instinctive urge to run.

As I quickly pulled some of these choice tidbits out of my memory bank for Tim's benefit—flipping them over like the pages in a photograph album—he started to laugh.

"Good God!" he exclaimed, "some of those places we stayed in gave us an overdose of Nature at her naked worst. They were the ones, though, that took most kindly to children."

"And with good reason," I agreed. "Let's face it: children are a lot like little untamed animals, messy, noisy, cranky, over-exuberant and often nuisances. Give them a strange dining room and they throw up; give them a different bed, and they won't sleep. Who wants that?"

"We didn't," Tim recalled. "Remember how tired we got of rusticating with Debbie in tourist cabins, farms and seaside shanties far off the beaten path?" He paused for a moment, and then we both exploded with the code word "Mountainvale" at the exact same moment—a word that promptly reduced us to near hysteria.

Mountainvale Hotel and Country Club was our one disastrous experiment with luxury class accommodations, when Debbie was about two years old. It was sleek and well-dressed in trim white stucco with green accessories, and it sat contentedly upon the succulent landscape like a rich, smug matron at a Newport picnic. A sign raised over the middle of the road announced it properly in well-modulated, Old English lettering, and it was definitely—even at first glance—as lush as a chinchilla coat.

No sooner had we settled into our luxurious room for the purpose of changing our clothes for dinner than we were forced to deal with the first major mishap of that unforgettable week-end: Where was Debbie?

"But she was beside me just minutes ago," I told Tim frantically. "Could she have wandered out into the hall?"

A loud howling at this point solved the mystery. Debbie was imprisoned in the bathroom and could not be gotten out because the lock was inexplicably jammed. Thereafter, it took three workmen supervised by the hotel manager and a fair turnout of curious guests—with Debbie screaming all the time—to cut the lock off, rescue Debbie, repair the mechanism and replace it: an overall kind of commotion that made everyone look at us as if we had set off some cheap firecrackers in their otherwise peaceful and dignified midst.

Somewhat daunted after this, and definitely shaken, we calmed Debbie, put on our formal gear, which we had not worn since our honeymoon, and headed for the dining room. It was all so much like a stage set with thick carpets, long terraces, drooping willows, beautiful clothes and low-keyed chattering that Tim and I felt like actors in hired evening dress. It was truly a propitious moment to brandish a ten-inch cigarette and say something appropriately dramatic, like, "Why, Cedric, I haven't seen you since Paris!"

The mood lasted all throughout the elaborate dinner. Soft candlelight lit up the tables and an orchestra played sentimental songs at the end of the big, shadowy room. The combination of soft lights, sweet music and long skirts made all of the females in the place feel like a cross between Mary Tyler Moore and Helen of Troy, while the men as obviously were bringing their Don Juan tendencies out of mothballs. Even the food seemed especially good, although I suspect that after a girl is married, anything she doesn't cook herself tastes wonderful. Then—it happened.

The waitress placed the hot teapot on the table; Debbie reached for it before we could intervene; and the boiling water poured over the entire front side of her little body. Debbie screamed with pain. Tim and I jumped up to lift her off her raised chair, literally tearing her clothes off in an effort to remove the source of the burning. It was bedlam! One chair got knocked over in our frenzied response; nearby diners ran over to see what was happening; the orchestra stopped playing; and Tim and I dashed through the gathering crowd—like football players down the field—to get upstairs and immerse Debbie in a tub of cold water.

When it was all over and Debbie—somehow miraculously unharmed—had been soothed, bribed with ice cream, and put to bed, Tim asked, somewhat hesitantly, "Do you want to take another crack at living it up? We could try the garden or the lounge. With Debbie asleep, either ought to be safe."

We settled for the garden. It was a beautiful, warmish night. The crickets were not too noisy, only mildly cheerful like someone humming a quiet song. There was that fragrant country smell of trees and flowers and cut grass and fresh breezes. The darkness was thick and soft and black, except for a skinny piece of moon in the sky.

"Isn't it beautiful?" I whispered to Tim.

"You are," he replied softly, putting his arms around me and holding me close.

On this amorous note, we stole quietly back into our room after a little while, feeling almost intoxicated with the heady romance in the air. Suddenly, though, there was a loud thud that froze us—like Lot's wife when she turned around—into two pillars of salt: Debbie had fallen out of her chaired-in bed.

Once again, we were disturbers of the peace. Debbie, awakened so abruptly and painfully out of a sound sleep, made more noise than a pack of coyotes baying at the moon. We received an irate phone call from the front desk, asking that we cease and desist—as if a crying child can be turned off at will like a faucet. Somebody knocked at our hotel door and reminded us angrily that it was nearly midnight. In the end, we could scarcely wait for the first glimpse of dawn to silently fold our tents and slip soundlessly away, before some well-heeled bounty hunter could turn us in.

"Boy, oh boy!" Tim finally managed to say through his laughter. "That week-end was our first and last lesson·in learning that children and glamour are like oil and water: They don't mix."

"Which is exactly what I've been trying to tell you," I responded triumphantly. "It isn't irresponsibility that makes Debbie want to get away alone with Pete. We had the same urges. It's just that it's hard to maintain a man and woman love-relationship when you're busy being a couple of parents. You've got to understand their side of it, too."

"So I understand." Tim was all serious again. "And what about our side of it? Are you going to let your understanding of Debbie's situation turn us into a pair of baby-sitters? Good grief, honey, is that what you're getting at now?"

"Nope." I went over and sat on Tim's lap. "It may be hard for Debbie at times, but it was for us when we were in that boat also. Yet we survived. And this is our time to be free and to enjoy the luxury of nothingness—if that's what we choose."

"Great!" Tim gave me a big kiss. "Then will you please tell her that we're no longer available?" he pleaded. "You've been saying that you would, ever since Melinda was born and you're still 'Chicken.' That baby's over three!"

"I'll tell her," I promised, "the very next time she asks."

The very next time Debbie asked was the very next day.

"If you and Daddy have no plans for Friday night," she telephoned as usual, "is it all right if we bring Melinda over? Pete and I are just aching to drop in at that new Disco in town!"

"No." I said the word quickly, firmly, before I could weaken. (I often wonder if our children realize how hard it

131

is for us to have to turn them down!)

For a moment there was a stunned silence. Then Debbie rallied. "Are you kidding?" she asked.

"Sweetie," I answered, hoping against all hope that she would understand our point of view as we did hers, "your father and I just don't like being tied down these days. We know how important getting out by yourselves is for you and Pete, because we went through the same kind of thing when we were raising you. But we think we have a right to our freedom now—before we're too old for it to matter anyway."

There was another pause. "But Mother," Debbie exclaimed, as uncomprehending as if I had been speaking literally in Greek. "What difference does it make if you have Melinda in the house when you're at home for the evening?"

"It makes a difference," I spoke patiently. "Even if we have nothing specific arranged, we like to be able to dash out—even if it's for nothing more than one of those hot-fudge sundaes over at Howard Johnson's. Have you any idea how many times we've had to refuse impromptu invitations because we were stuck here with Melinda?"

"Stuck with Melinda?" Debbie was as outraged as a five-year-old who hears someone say there is no Santa Claus. "But Mother, I thought you and Daddy loved Melinda."

"We do love Melinda." The session was as bad as I had known it would be. "It's got nothing to do with loving Melinda. We just don't want to baby-sit her anymore—unless, of course, something special or an emergency comes up. That's different, naturally."

"But I thought you enjoyed Melinda." Debbie was almost crying—and so was I.

"We do." I swallowed my tears and tried for a light tone. "She's a delight, but as you know only too well, also a chore. Maybe when we retire and are really old, we won't object to minding our grandchildren. But we're both too busy now to be ready to settle down yet."

My feeble attempt at humor was wasted on Debbie.

"Pete's mother and father are only too happy to take Melinda whenever we ask," she persisted.

"I know." And I did. How many times had I heard Mrs. Driscoll's great funny: "I'm always happy when Melinda comes—and always happy to see her go!" Debbie had heard it frequently, too, but apparently it did not tell her what it told me.

This last realization ended the conversation as far as I was concerned. Was it the eternal Generation Gap or the crazy mismatch of parents and children that makes heredity seem as unpredictable as what comes out of a slot machine? I opted for the former and said, "Look, sweetie, maybe you'll never understand how your father and I feel until you're a grandparent yourself. But it's how we feel."

"Well." Debbie drew her pride around her as if it were an ermine wrap. "I'm glad you told me. And don't worry, Mother. You can tell Daddy we won't bother you with our baby anymore."

Exit Debbie—for four whole weeks.

I called her many times in the interval and she even called me. There was a distance between us, however, that could never be measured in miles. We exchanged health bulletins and the usual tidbits of family news, but the old, easy laughter and repartee were gone.

"Is she still angry because we won't baby-sit?" Tim asked one night when we were discussing the fact that Debbie had not popped in even once in three whole weeks.

"Angry—or hurt," I replied sadly. "Sweetie, do you think we should have held our peace?"

"No." Tim was definite.

"But I don't want a breach," I said worriedly. "I miss Debbie. I miss Melinda. I even miss Pete."

Tim laughed at the last. "Honey," he said, "you are in a bad way."

I had to laugh, too. In-lawship is always a slow and difficult business, and Pete's adjustment to us was still in the

133

embryonic stage. Actually, it took ten years before he could call Tim and me Mother and Dad in a way that didn't sound as if the words were lines he had difficulty in remembering for his part in a school play.

"But I mean it," I finally returned to the subject. "I feel awful about the whole thing. Debbie doesn't understand what I was trying to say. She just thinks we're rejecting her and her child. How can this ugliness end?"

It ended abruptly—but never completely—one week later. That fourth week of Debbie's Distant Treatment was especially painful for me because the Saturday at the end of it was my birthday. Ordinarily, since Debbie was married, she had had a family dinner for the occasion that made the day a very special one for all of us. This time there was no mention even to indicate that she remembered the date that was coming up.

"Stop moping," Tim consoled me. "I'll take you out for a real celebration myself."

Saturday came and I went into a total decline: no word from Debbie. I had alienated my daughter for life.

"You get all dressed up, do you hear?" Tim commanded, when I was still sitting around forlornly at five o'clock. "It's your birthday and we're going out."

Unwillingly, I stood up to obey—and the front door bell rang. "I'll get the door," Tim said, hurrying out, "and you go on up. Come on, honey, it's getting late."

As I stood hesitantly in the living room, I could hear Tim's voice. It echoed through the hallway.

"Debbie! Pete!" My heart jumped when I listened to his greeting. "Come on in! We've missed you!"

Even while he was speaking, Melinda came running into the living room and almost knocked me over with an exuberant hug.

"Grandmuzzer! Grandmuzzer!" Her excitement was enchanting. "Mamma made you a birthday cake like you like—with lots and lots of butter. And I helped! And it's to say Happy Birthday!"

134

I was so busy hugging Melinda back that I didn't look up until Debbie was in the room also, standing there with a big pie plate on which sat a round layer cake with pink and white icing.

"Happy Birthday, Mother," she said, with a tremulous smile.

That was all. But it was everything.

"Oh, Debbie!" I could have wept for joy. Instead, I tried to put my arms around her and almost knocked the cake out of her hands—which made us all laugh.

"Hey, hold it!" Tim exclaimed as he rushed over and rescued the pan. "O.K. Now you can kiss and make up."

This time, we held each other tightly in our arms.

"I've missed you," she said.

"I've missed you," I replied, "and I love you very much."

"And I love you, Mother," she answered. "No matter what."

She meant it. She really did—but there was no understanding in her heart. It was just a truce and that was all it could ever be. Poor Debbie was stuck with anomalous parents who had rejected their grandparental role: They would not baby-sit. It was apparently still a terrible, incredible fact in her mind but she was nobly, forebearingly prepared to live with it because there was nothing she could do about it.

Nor was there—and this final realization was sudden and swift and sure in my mind even as I held her close and regretted the gulf that would always be between us—anything that I could do about it either.

Chapter VIII

TRIAL BY FIRE

GRANDPARENTHOOD, like parenthood, is without reprieve. Once the physical relationship has been established, it is a psychological fact of life that you will never again be free from the sense of concern and responsiveness to need that were equally inescapable throughout your previous role as a parent. You may quarrel with your grown sons and daughters, you may refuse to baby-sit for their children, you may have little or no communication with either: but you can no more be divorced from any of them than you can from your own self. When the Prodigal returns, then out comes the Fatted Calf—as automatically and immediately as a pre-set oil burner flips on when the temperature drops. When the alarm is sounded, when the cry is heard, then the battle stations are manned with all the reflex rapidity of a submarine crew in enemy waters responding to an attack.

As usual with all my lessons in grandparenthood, I learned about this the hard way. With the detente in our baby-sitting confrontation came a resurgent feeling of full and final release that was as delusive as it was delightful. For all of almost twelve more months, in fact, I was honestly convinced that at long last, Tim and I had achieved a true measure of independence—even though with some re-

137

grettable aftermath as in any Civil War.

"Do you realize," I pointed out to Tim one night, several weeks after my birthday, "that Debbie hardly ever drops in anymore, now that we no longer baby-sit for Melinda?"

Tim sighed. "I've noticed," he said. Then he added, "Do you think she's still upset?"

"In a way," I answered. "But to be really fair about it, she is mighty busy, you know."

Debbie had taken a part-time nursing job at the local hospital. That her days were fully occupied was beyond dispute.

"Too busy to see us?" Tim persisted.

"Too busy to waste time coming by here when there's nothing special in it for her." I kept my tone of voice matter-of-fact. "Most of her flitting in and out before stemmed from the business of dropping Melinda off or picking her up. Now, when they get a sitter, she and Pete head out by themselves or else with their own friends." I paused, then started to laugh. "Good God!" I exclaimed, as the idea hit me. "Maybe that's why most grandparents baby-sit so much. How else can they get to see their children and grandchildren?"

Tim joined in my laughter. Then he sobered.

"Honey," he asked, all serious again, "do you mind this cold-shoulder bit?"

"It's not a cold-shoulder bit," I protested. "It's just the way of things. Debbie's grown up and away. She has her own life to lead and it basically doesn't include us."

"But do you mind?" A lawyer-husband can be positively painful at times when a simple conversation gets transformed into a full-scale cross-examination.

"I mind." I made the admission reluctantly, having until that moment resisted any real analysis of the phenomenon. "Why shouldn't I mind? Oh, I know: the robins kick their young out of the nest, and we're supposed to let go, too. But I'm not a robin. I'm a human being. Why are we supposed to equate ourselves with the birds and the beasts?

138

The Bible assures us that man is special. Even the evolutionists recognize an upward trend. "Yes," I finished emphatically, "I mind. And I always will."

"Well, so do I." Tim's prompt concurrence surprised me. "We were a family unit and Debbie was a very, very important part of it. But you're right. This is the way the cookie crumbles and we've just got to adjust. It was only the two of us in the beginning, and it's the two of us in the end. It takes some getting used to, doesn't it? But honestly, honey, there are a lot of plusses in this stage of the game also."

And there were.

A new kind of warmth and understanding grew between Tim and me. We each worked harder in our own way: I began accepting lecture engagements beyond the narrow radius I had adhered to when Debbie was home, and Tim began to assume responsibility for out-of-town cases that he had previously avoided. Whenever possible, we accompanied each other out "into the field"; and whenever impossible, the quiet but deep joy of each reunion made us feel with each homecoming the way the Pilgrims must have felt when they landed on Plymouth Rock. It was wonderful!

Even our missing Debbie in our lives—which we did and still do—became another bond between us. We travelled—sometimes literally to nowhere—and we visited around frequently and we collapsed ultimately in the incomparable luxury of nothingness, but there were inevitable times when the void that used to be filled with Debbie would surface suddenly and sadly.

"But I'm really getting used to being apart from her," I boasted to Tim several months later, when we were driving over to Cleveland one day for a concert. "I used to hang up after each telephone conversation with Debbie and almost want to cry because she seemed so far off. Not that it was ever anything that she said—just a deep sense of apartness. But thank God, I don't get down like that anymore."

Actually, our grandparental role at this time had more or

139

less shaped up into a recognizable pattern, if not a completely satisfying one. Telephone contact kept us abreast of what was going on in a general kind of way with Debbie and Pete and Melinda. Admittedly, it was often like walking into the theatre in the middle of a play, and then trying to fill in everything that happened before from the subsequent dialogue—but it was better than nothing.

Occasionally, too, we did manage some direct contact by inviting the three Driscolls over for Sunday dinner. For Debbie, such an invitation was usually irresistible because it offered her an opportunity to escape cooking; and knowing this, I was never above taking advantage of it. Surely, this kind of subtle manipulation to arrange a get-together was much to be preferred over a blunt "How come we hardly ever see you these days?" accusation with all of its attendant recrimination, protestation, rationalization and enduring irritation.

The essentially one-way deal in this direct-contact area, incidentally, was another source of secret frustration for Tim and me. While Debbie still had a key to our house and our upgrudging acceptance of her prerogative to come and go freely, we were made unceasingly aware that her house was hers—not ours. She could invade our closets and our refrigerator with impunity, but we would no more even have gone to her place without a definite invitation—which she was generally too busy to extend—than we would have thought of barging in at the White House. There was no clear-cut delineation of this state of affairs, only a tacit acknowledgement of the fact by all concerned. Wherefore: The Sunday-Dinner-At-Grandmother's routine emerged as the occasional alternative to absolute isolation.

Another ploy that was utilized to achieve the same objective in that never-ending, always exasperating and sometimes amusing War of Nerves which is waged generation against generation on the grandparental level, was the Family-Gathering-For-A-Holiday theme. There is an unwritten law in our land, apparently, that mandates a clannish celebration of Christmas and Easter and Thanksgiving. It has nothing to do with religion, mind you, and it's probably just a vestigial social custom left over from earlier Americana, but it does ensure that parents can expect and usually receive visits on these specified days from their children and grandchildren.

Let me confess here and now that my observances in this regard, during that period when my withdrawal symptoms from Debbie were most acute, became almost fanatical. Each appropriate date was circled in blood on my calendar. It did not matter to me then that poor Debbie's attempts to cut herself meticulously into equal halves between Pete's family and hers for these occasions would have stumped a Solomon. I was incredibly unmoved at that time by the obviously compulsory nature of the ritualistic attendance which had some of the uncomfortable earmarks of a traffic court appearance in response to a summons for a moving violation. All I knew and cared about—after orgies of preparation—was that briefly but blissfully we were all together again as a family. And in my underlying yearning for this to be, I insisted adamantly upon my pound of flesh.

Of course, there were times when we did take Melinda for an afternoon or an evening when something urgent came up suddenly and Debbie couldn't get a sitter. It was not a frequent occurrence, though, and both Tim and I came away from it usually with a sad awareness of the distance that was inherent between our little granddaughter and ourselves.

Melinda was a lovely child—with Debbie's fair coloring and Pete's sweet smile. She was bright and quick in her responses, and such a reminder of how Debbie had been at the same age that it was difficult at times to remember that she was not Debbie.

"Grandmother," she inquired typically once, shortly before her fourth birthday, "if God made everyone. . ." then she interrupted herself abruptly to ask, "Didn't he?"

"He did," I replied.

141

"Then who made God?"

Her questions—as Debbie's had been in the long ago—were endless and intriguing.

"I think," she told me seriously one day, apropos of nothing that I knew about, "that if the only way you can tell a boy from a girl without clothes on is by looking for a jigger, then why didn't God make a more polite way?"

Another time, she accosted me with, "My friend Tina's mother had a baby and mamma told me how it works. But you know, Grandmother, I don't think I'll like hatching eggs."

It was such a happy reminder of Debbie—and yet, not for a single moment could we really forget that it was not Debbie. When Melinda said or did something that was in contradiction of what we had done in raising Debbie, we felt constrained to voice no comment. What this meant, in effect, was that we had to exercise the same self-restraint with the small child that we had learned to adhere to painfully in our interaction with our grown daughter. This tended to undermine the spontaneity and warmth that should have, but decidedly did not, permeate our relationship.

"Don't you see?" I explained to Tim one night after Melinda had left. "I fully recognize that Debbie can do as she chooses to do with her own child. It's just that I don't want to come in the middle, or make Melinda have to weigh one point of view against the other. That's an unfair burden to place on someone who's practically still a baby. Her loyalties shouldn't be split and they rightfully belong with her mother."

"I know exactly what you mean," Tim agreed. "Did you notice today how Melinda chimed in on all the T.V. commercials, as if every indoor waking moment is spent in front of the set?"

"And how we both kept mum," I added ruefully.

In our day—even before the current escalation of sex, brutality and terror—Debbie's television watching had been strictly censored. Not that I personally abhorred much of the viewing menu. Westerns, for example, were and are amazingly innocuous. A Western hero is notoriously, boringly, a Good Samaritan and militant saint. He is consistently more virtuous and admirable than the leading man in a soap opera, with all of these homespun qualities wrapped up in a body like the Apollo Belvedere's, a mind like Socrates', and a punch like Muhammad Ali's. As for the plot—that unvarying, repetitious plan of action which has not changed one iota from my childhood to now—it also is as exemplary as a Bible story.

Mysteries, similarly (of which there were constant servings), were equal models of moral behavior. Who could quarrel with a basic pattern that was as rigid as any Western theme? Right inevitably makes might; evil is smashed; and murderers will out.

Nevertheless, we had felt a strong responsibility to maintain unrelenting vigilance over Debbie's T.V. time. In the first place, there is more blood spilled hourly on television than was ever spilled annually in the entire McCoy-Hatfield feud. In the second place, television can become a serious addiction. It is definitely, dangerously habit forming. It is an escape. It is a twentieth-century Siren Song that lures us all away from petty cares and bothersome chores of our little lives to the glamorous, never-never Land of the Lotus Eaters where even grown-ups—much less children—cease doing things on a constructive, active, personal basis, but sit instead, bemused and drugged and entranced, while only the pictures move on.

The discipline exerted in the realm of television, however, was only symptomatic of the overall discipline with which Debbie was raised. The rash statements that used to explode from her, consequently, in moments of angry frustration, should have forewarned us—but didn't—as to the kind of mother she would someday be. If half of the Utopia she planned to dwell in when she grew up were to be believed, Debbie, as an adult, would never wash, never go to sleep, never turn off the television, and never stop at less than six scoops of ice cream at one time.

Apparently, we never did succeed in teaching her that the difference between discipline in childhood and age is that it becomes self-administered. Instead, her approach to Melinda was a laissez faire one that included almost every single aspect of her daughter's life.

Melinda, for example, was openly hooked on T.V. Instead of Little Bo Peep and Humpty Dumpty, her earliest repertoire encompassed such things as the Pepsi Generation jingle and Duz Does Everything. Her favorite baby-sitter—because she so insisted—was a young woman who usually came to sit with her illegitimate baby for which, I was frequently informed, "There is no Daddy, because Susie never got married."

Melinda's religion, in the same way, was vague and totally unconfining, "She'll come to her own conclusions when she gets older," said Debbie. Melinda was never spanked either, it being exceedingly clear that Debbie belonged to that vast segment of the American population which regards even the mild slap on a child's hand (when he's discovered about to turn in a false alarm or steal the dimes from a blind man's cup) as unadulterated child abuse.

"It's none of our business," Tim would remind me firmly on those infrequent baby-sitting occasions when we would be exposed to Melinda and I would wince in silence at some of her telltale remarks and actions.

"I know it's none of our business," I would concede with annoyance whenever we were alone. "But where does it leave us anyway? If Melinda were Kay Lemle's granddaughter down the street, I wouldn't give two cents of a hoot at what she did or said. Am I supposed to be as removed and unmoved as if she were a strange child who happened to stop by? Is that what being a grandparent has come to be?"

Apparently, it had.

Familial peace, therefore, was more easily maintained by the working relationship we had shifted into with Debbie.

The fewer encounters Tim and I had with her meant there were fewer opportunities for eruptions. When we did meet, after gaps of uninvolvement, it became comparatively easier for us to stand like the plastic figures on a wedding cake and make only the proper, expected grandparental noises: we could smile, we could applaud, we could cluck our tongues sympathetically.

Little by little, there was a lessening urge to explode at Debbie in response to some of Melinda's uninhibited tantrums with, "So what's wrong with a little frustration anyway? Civilization is one inhibition after another, practiced by the many for the good of all. Sooner or later, every unfrustrated, uncivilized child will have a rude awakening when he struggles to cope with reality!" Gradually, definitely, I could sense such a dwindling of personal projection into Debbie's existence, that I found myself no longer spouting forth even inside me at some of her maternal management with something like, "Why do you treat Melinda like an honored house guest instead of a member of the family? Why shouldn't she learn to make her own bed and clean up? She'll have to take her share of K.P. when she grows up. Let her get used to the real facts of life now!"

"Sweetie," I told Tim with a sincere sense of satisfaction, after several months had elapsed in this fashion, "I would never have believed it possible for me to move out of Debbie's range as far as I've come. For years, I've focused my attention mostly on Debbie. To a great extent we both have. I just never thought I could really do it. Did you?"

"You had to do it," Tim reminded me. "It seems to be the only way to maintain even superficial harmony in the family. After all, necessity is the mother of invention. Right?"

"But desperation is its father," I replied laughingly.

Most times, in everyday life, unfortunately, need in itself is not enough to spark human imagination into creative fire. There must be something else—some greater force, some overwhelming desire, some basic primitive drive for the preservation of our very lives or any little comfortable part of it—that impels us out of our natural lethargy into defensive action. Then, and usually only then, are all things truly possible, and behold, another innovation is accomplished—as with me and Debbie!

"You know, Sweetie," I went on aloud for Tim's benefit, "it does seem regrettable that as grandparents, we have to break what's left of the Silver Cord for our own protection. People usually talk of children having to do it to escape parental clutches. What we're doing is less popularized but as basic."

"Maybe it's just an extension of the Generation Gap," Tim suggested. "A grandchild introduces still another generation into the picture and complicates the whole idea. It may be an exacerbation of the Generation Gap, but it's not necessarily any more unnatural than the original one was."

I found the idea consoling.

Certainly, before Melinda, the Generation Gap, as such, had never bothered me. To begin with, the whole business must be unquestionably as old as Adam and Eve's first confrontation with their Cain and Abel. In my own experience, for instance, I can still remember hearing my mother's generation complain about their parents' horrified reactions to the advent of lipstick and "bobbed hair" and the Black Bottom. Nor was I so old as yet that I could not vividly recall my own burning adolescent conviction that my parents were nothing but a bunch of frustrating *old, old* people who had antideluvian notions about everything from how tight a skirt should be, and how much make-up was proper for a "decent girl," to the acceptable time a Saturday night date should be over. Nor—since it was only yesterday, so to speak—could I forget Debbie's pubescent (and probably present) certainty that I was an "old-fashioned ultra-conservative" whose opinions stemmed from somewhere between the Stone Age and the Flood.

Accordingly, I had always recognized that the Generation Gap was not only nothing new, but equally nothing unnatural. I could never understand why so many people treated it like a dreadful disease for which massive campaigns like the March of Dimes on Birth Defects should be launched. How could we possibly expect young people to see life from the same vantage point that their parents do? By what great illogic do we ask our children to accept calmly some of the hard truths that we took years in coming to terms with ourselves?

Not that the inevitability of the Generation Gap makes it any easier to bear—as every generation in its turn can testify! Not, either, that the manifestations these days aren't alarmingly extreme—although I can remember similar shades of idealism and radicalism from my own youth, all mixed up somewhere with much talk of free love, trial marriage and political despair. The fact is that the Generation Gap is and has always been a definite but bearable thorn in the side of every set of parents and children. There are times when the distance between the two can seem greater than from here to the Moon. There are other times when they view each other like two enemy camps, dug in on opposite sides of a "No Man's Land" river. On the whole, though, the dominant feeling in each group is a basic kind of understanding that there is no underlying malice involved—a reluctant sort of forbearance that stems from the instinctive recognition that "that's just the way they are"—and these, in turn, make the whole impasse comparatively endurable.

It had been this way, at least, in all of our earlier skirmishes with Debbie throughout the years when she was growing up. So—if Tim were right and what we were experiencing now was an extension and intensification of the old, familiar Generation Gap on a grandparental level, why couldn't we laugh while we groaned at it the way we did before?"

"Because," Tim speculated, when I presented him with this puzzle, "we're older; because we hoped we'd have a meeting of the minds with Debbie sooner rather than later; because even when we fought with Debbie, she was still

147

our child, but now the disagreements are keeping Melinda from really being our grandchild—and all that grandparent propaganda that we've been hearing for ages makes us feel we're being short-changed as grandparents." Tim paused for breath. "Honey," he said finally, "I'm only guessing. Who really knows? In any case, though, I'm proud of your adjustment. Instead of moping and complaining, you've made a life apart from Debbie. You're really free."

I was proud of myself, too. We sat there for a while longer, closer than two slices of bread on a sandwich—with pure, fallacious reasoning in between. We sat there, and never even realized the most fundamental fact of all in the whole grandparenthood routine: That you are never free.

I should have sensed this in the months after our babysitting ultimatum when I had been working out my emancipation. In retrospect, I can clearly see at the time what I missed: That although Debbie seemed contented enough with the separate courses we pursued in our own ways, she wanted and expected moral support, sympathy and help whenever something went wrong.

"Oh, Mother! My sitter's not coming and I'm due at work by one o'clock. What'll I do?"

"Mother! My car has some kind of leak in the radiator and it won't go! The man said it would cost a hundred dollars at least to fix it! And he needs the car for a whole day!"

"We've been looking at houses, Mother! Melinda is getting too cooped up in this little apartment. We need more space. I just don't know how we can swing the down payment!"

Whatever it was, Debbie's plaintive voice over the phone was never hesitant about regaling me with the worst. I, in turn, was never hesitant about responding with my best, as if I were a robot whose switch had been turned on—that is, in the beginning. Time, cars, money, encouragement, sympathy—name it and I gave it or did it because it was Debbie; because I had been so doing for Debbie even before she was able to express her own wants.

Sometimes, the doing and the giving caused considerable upheaval in our lives. On one such memorable occasion Debbie took my car; I took Tim's—and by the time we picked her up from the repair shop and put all the others in their proper places again, Tim had waited one hour on the courthouse steps when his trial ended earlier than anticipated, and I ran from a lecture hall without a Question and Answer Session that had been promised the audience.

Another treasured time occurred when Debbie's frantic S.O.S. reached me just as I was about to leave for the Creative Writing class I teach at the college. In my then state of mind, I wound up taking Melinda to the school with me, where I parked her in an adjacent empty classroom under the watchful eye of a freshman whom I shanghaied from the library. Thereafter, through the open transom, came the sounds of hectic enjoyment as Melinda's entranced keeper amused her (and himself) by wiggling his ears and making faces and chasing her up and down the aisles. What a fiasco! My voice climbed up to be heard while everyone looked about with vague annoyance, as if to determine the culprit; and I—to conclusively remove myself from even the remotest connection with this outrage— looked more affronted than the rest.

"This has got to stop," Tim decreed one evening when I was briefing him on the latest. "Debbie can't have it both ways. We're never supposed to comment—much less interfere! She's a grown-up woman and she has a husband: but let something happen and she yells for Mother and Daddy to bail her out the way she expected us to when she was ten years old. And you," he finished accusingly, "oblige."

"But what else can I do?" I asked seriously.

"You can say No." Tim was just as serious.

"It's not that easy," I replied. "Sweetie, we've been looking out for Debbie ever since when. She's still my child, even if we're not as close as we were. Don't you see?"

"I do see." Tim was adamant. "Look, honey, I know the whole relationship is not simple to analyze. And I know that she turns to us for help because way deep down she still feels she can because we are her parents. . ."

"Do you really think she does?" I interrupted wistfully.

"Of course she does," he stated emphatically. "Why, just the other day, Pete dropped in at the office to ask me to draw up his and Debbie's wills. They think they should have one. And who do you think they've decided should have guardianship of Melinda in case he and Debbie were to die in a common disaster?" Tim paused for effect. Then he said, with a flourish, "You and I."

"Oh, Tim!" I was genuinely moved. "Even though she goes off in the opposite direction from us on everything?"

"Even though," he affirmed. "According to Pete, Debbie persuaded him about this choice because 'no matter what,' we are 'reliable and intelligent and loving.' Those very words."

It made me want to cry. "That's the most daughterly accolade I've heard from Debbie in a long time."

"I know," Tim agreed. "And don't let it go to your head. Of course, she feels that we're her parents and that she can count on us. But it's a new kind of ballgame now. She doesn't want us in her life in an ordinary way because she can stand on her own two feet. Well, she can't expect us to pop round anytime anything extraordinary happens. You've got to learn to say No."

"O.K. I'll try." The concession made me unhappy.

"Honey." Tim came over and sat down beside me. "I know it's hard." He held me close. "But remember this: Part of your helping is because you love Debbie. A big part of it, though, is that by being available for help, it gives you some involvement in her life—even if mostly in times of stress—and it's also a way to make you of some importance to Debbie. But if we're really going to follow the general 'hands-off' path we're already on with her, it's got to include this. It's unfair of her to suddenly expect to resume our old relationship when she needs something, but to go blithely on her way when all is well."

I had never really thought of it like that at all. After some reflection, I did realize that Tim was right. Whereupon, I promptly and firmly decide to learn to say No.

The trouble in the subsequent learning, unfortunately, was that whenever Debbie expressed a need, I was "all systems go." It was the most fundamental, elemental, simple reflex action. Stopping myself, therefore, was like pulling the brake cord on a train that is moving at ninety miles an hour; and it always left me as shaken.

Still, I persevered.

"I'm sorry, dear," I began making myself say to Debbie. "Your father's tied up and so am I. Have you tried Pete's mother?"

"That's a shame, Debbie," I would reply sincerely. "We can't spare a car, though, because Daddy and I each have commitments."

"I'd love to help, sweetie." I was always pleasant but honest. "But if I stop to pick Melinda up from nursery school and then drive the hour more back here, I'll be late for my talk at the Women's Club."

It was truly a difficult thing for me to do. What made it even worse was the fact that neither Debbie nor I discussed it openly. It remained—and remains—one of those moot questions in our lives which probably no amount of argument or analysis would have resolved anyway: as pointed and pointless as, Which Came First, the Chicken or the Egg?; or Who Was There, the Lady or the Tiger?

At first, Debbie would react to each one of my refusals with a stunned silence followed by a shocked "Oh." I, in turn, would try to cover up the awkward pause by a line of chatter, just as a veteran auctioneer keeps on talking while the merchandise is being brought up for bids. Eventually, of course, we both achieved comparative ease in our respective roles. Debbie, although obviously disappointed, would say, "Oh well; no harm in trying"; I, although still somewhat ill at ease, would respond with, "Let me know how you make out, sweetie."

151

"I've done it! I've done it!" I finally announced to Tim delightedly. "I'm still not exactly comfortable about saying No to Debbie, but at least I can do it. I help her only when it's convenient for me to do so, and I no longer think I have to apologize or feel guilty when I don't. I don't even worry about it, either."

"You shouldn't." Tim looked at me approvingly. "If it's Hands-Off that she wants, it's got to be Hands-Off all the way. She can't have it both ways."

It sounded logical and it sounded fine, but it wasn't true. In grandparenthood, as in parenthood, it can never be Hands-Off all the way.

The denouement came exactly two weeks later.

"Mother?" Debbie's voice over the phone had an unfamiliar sound.

"Debbie?" I asked, just to be sure.

"Oh, Mother!" Debbie was crying. "It's Melinda. She's got pneumonia. Bad. We're taking her to the hospital now."

This time Debbie hadn't asked for anything. She didn't have to. Underlying all of the bravado, all of the independence talk on both sides, I knew in that very moment that there was a bond between us that nothing on earth could ever break. I didn't know exactly what it was, and I couldn't understand why it should have survived the tension and turbulence in our relationship throughout the last few years. I only knew that it was a fact of our lives and would always be.

When I could talk again, I said simply, "We'll meet you at the hospital, dear," and hung up.

Not even fleetingly did it occur to me—or to Tim, for that matter—not to go. We could have awaited word in the comfort of our own home. We could have gone the next morning. Debbie hadn't even really asked us to come. There was nothing practical that we could do. We were going, nonetheless, because our child and her child were in trouble and their trouble was our own. This kind of identification is the taproot of parenthood as well as grandparenthood, and I have never disputed it since.

The week that followed has all the haziness in my mind of an opium eater's nightmare. Debbie, to begin with, needed constant bolstering and I bolstered. Her nursing background, unfortunately, was a great hindrance in establishing any real calm in her mind. As with most medical families that I have known, her philosophy of personal doctoring—particularly since Melinda had been born—had been as indeterminable as the Irish Sweepstakes and as paradoxical as caviar in the Automat. In ordinary matters, her care for Melinda made the delinquent cobbler with his shoeless children seem like a paternal philanthropist; in times of actual illness, her concern and fear were magnified beyond normal proportions. She would scorn the routine colds and minor complaints that are only nine-tenths of the common ailments of daily living for any child, but given a genuine symptom, she was always unrestrainable. Every earache Melinda had ever suffered, had been viewed as an imminent mastoid, and every mongrel gas pain had filled her with bloody visions of acute appendicitis.

Now, in the face of Melinda's full-blown pneumonia, she was utterly, predictably inconsolable.

"But honey," Pete and Tim and I told her, "there are so many wonder drugs now for pneumonia. She'll be all right."

"They don't always work," Debbie's response was consistent. "There are resistant strains that kill."

Poor Debbie! The curse of possession is the fear of loss. And the dread is greatest when it concerns those whom we hold most dearly in our hearts. I knew only too well what she was feeling. You can rarely raise a child without going through these Gesthsemanes.

My next self-imposed chore was maintaining an aura of normalcy for Melinda. This was exceedingly hard for me to do because I hate hospitals. Walking into one, as far as I have always been concerned, is like entering a world as alien and appalling as a Star Wars set. The sight—even in passing—of that gruesome equipment is disturbing to me;

and the odor—that nauseating, anesthetizing, hard-to-breathe, antiseptic smell, has a thoroughly demoralizing effect.

For Melinda's sake, though, I was prepared to pretend we had all come to Disneyland. Melinda was obviously as much afraid as I. She had a high fever; her face was flushed; her clear blue eyes were clouded over; and she had obvious difficulty breathing. She was disinterested in the toys we bought for her, and wanted someone with her every single minute, or else she howled. She wouldn't eat.

"I'll spell you, Debbie," I said, laying out a routine, "She's scared, you know. She needs someone close by her for reassurance. Let's humor her. Remember how we used to spoil you when you were sick when you were small?"

During illnesses, all the rules for Debbie's good behavior were always suspended. How important Debbie used to be as she lay unthroned in bed, delivering royal commands. Not one spoonful of medicine would she swallow without proper remuneration, which might be anything from an outlandish favor to a dollar bill. How reluctantly she would abdicate when she was completely recovered.

"I remember," Debbie answered with a small smile. "I even turned my talents to malingering at times, just to enjoy the good life." Debbie stopped abruptly. "Oh, Mother," she cried, clinging to me, "I'm so frightened. I love her so much. She just has to get well."

"She will get well," I said with all the assurance I could muster. "God hears our prayers."

"Mine, too?" she asked, and we both knew what she meant. "Because I have been praying."

"Yours, too," I answered, thinking wryly to myself: Verily, verily, there are no atheists in foxholes!

It was a long week and a terrible week. I practically moved into the hospital, as did Debbie and Pete. Tim was our link with the outside since (except for Pete's parents) no visitors were allowed; and he handled all the telephone inquiries. For all of us, though, it was like being in limbo—

that strange nowhere place that families retreat to in times of crises, when they have literally stopped the rest of the world and gotten off.

By the end of the fifth day, it was marvelously apparent that Melinda was on the mend. She was pale and weak, but definitely beginning to enjoy the whole fuss within the limits of her four-year-old intelligence.

"Was I very sick?" she asked eagerly, revelling in her featured role in Returned From the Dead. "Did I almost die?"

By the seventh day, she was in great sickroom form. She insisted upon and received five cents for every pill she swallowed (cheaper rates than Debbie's had been in her day), ice cream at least once with each meal in a wide range and choice of flavors, and cutouts and coloring books by the dozen.

She startled the nurses when they opened the door by pointing a toy gun at them and shouting, "Hands up or I'll shoot." She began to ring her call buzzer incessantly (even when we were right by her side) until the harried staff took it out of the room.

"She's about ready to go home," I told Tim wearily on the last hospital night. "Tomorrow."

We were sitting in the nearby waiting room together for a brief visit. Debbie and Pete were in with Melinda.

"And so are you," Tim replied. "Right now. You're exhausted."

"We're all exhausted," I corrected him. "It's been such an ordeal." I paused for a moment, in search of the thought I could feel glimmering in the back of my mind. "You know, sweetie, I've been thinking. I never dreamed I would get this worked up about Melinda."

"Was it Melinda?" Tim asked me seriously, "or was it Debbie whose hurt you were responding to?"

"Nope." I didn't have to search for my answer. "it was Debbie, too, of course, but it was mostly Melinda. Do you realize that this is the first time I've ever interacted with

155

that child, without stopping first to worry about what Debbie would say?"

"'That's because you knew Debbie was too upset and distracted to notice," Tim answered, grinning. He squeezed my hand hard. Then he continued, "I didn't know I cared so much, either," he admitted. "I only know that every part of me was focused on her getting well."

"I know," I agreed. "It was almost the way it used to feel when Debbie used to get sick. Remember when she was operated on for acute appendicitis? What was she then: four? five?"

"Four and a half." Tim was always good with facts and figures.

"Just a wee bit older than Melinda," I reflected. "But there is a difference between then and this time. I couldn't let go the way I used to. It was as if I had an obligation to keep my cool and provide moral support for everyone. Do you know what I mean?"

"You mean you're the grandmother now," Tim replied, "and not the mother. That's what made the difference. Anyhow, don't you realize that in some ways you've been doing this with every cold and fever Melinda's ever had? Even when Debbie hit the panic button because Melinda was a late talker, you kept reassuring her in every conversation that you hadn't said a word until you were two years old, so it must just be genetic. Thank God, Melinda's never had anything life-threatening before—which is why you're so aware of how you respond now. But honey," Tim concluded his analysis on a firm and serious note, "you do realize that when things simmer down to normal, nothing in our basic grandparental role will have changed."

I nodded, almost too worn out for more talk. How could Tim think I had any foolish illusions about any future togetherness? Of course, he was right! But there was more to it than that, anyway.

"Sweetie, I finally said, leaning against him contentedly, "I know nothing's changed, but I also know now that there is some kind of a bond between us and Melinda that is as indestructible as the one between us and Debbie. It's irrational in a way—because we are so much on the outside looking in—and there are bound to be times when we will resent it. But like it or not, fair or not—under the circumstances—it's there and it will always be. In fact," I finished suddenly, sitting up straight to share the revelation, "it was this bond probably—throughout this terrible past week—that made me feel like a real grandmother for the first time."

Chapter IX

GRADUATION DAY

THE PATH of the novice grandparent is fraught with innumerable pitfalls which, fortunately, he scarcely ever sees. His armor is ignorance, and the spur of his accomplishment is inexperience. Determination rather than knowledge carries the beginner far; and often it is only in retrospect that a true measure can be taken of the heroic adjustment that has finally been made.

The realization that I had in fact become a true "grandma" was something that came over me gradually in the weeks following Melinda's recovery. Not that our relationship was really altered. On the contrary, we slipped back into low gear as effortlessly and smoothly as an automatic transmission shifts speeds.

Something had happened, however, even though I wasn't sure exactly what it was. Illness had engulfed my whole grandparental life like a mighty Day of Judgment. It had swept into the pettiness of our everyday existence—the false pride, the superficial words, the careless replies—and it had stripped us bare of everything but the basic truths. It had been, temporarily (as it always is), one of the greatest common denominators a human being can know—and I had been effectively reduced: Melinda was my grandchild; I was her grandmother; I would always be her grandmother.

These were the facts and that was that.

"But what does it all mean?"

I directed this question at a group of guests one evening several weeks afterwards, when we were having a dinner party to celebrate my having just about finished this book. After months of keeping my nose practically glued to the literary grindstone, until my head was beginning to feel more emptied out than a last-week's pay envelope, I had decided to kill many of my social obligations off with one stone (and one roast) even as I commemorated the occasion. We had eaten our way through a meal that could have fed a herd of elephants, and were lazily sprawled around the living room, discussing my book, when we suddenly became a mini-Forum on Grandparenthood in response to my query.

"Let's really talk about it," Fred Shultz said. "I remember when you tried some discreet pumping way back when, Edwina. And Christine and I have been thinking about it on and off for some time. But let's really lay it out honestly now. What do you all say?"

Harry and Gwen Richards, who had also been present at our original session before I even began writing the book, laughed and nodded. My friend, Hilda Davis, and her Larry, agreed promptly, as did Janet and Stewart Scott.

"Do I get a vote?" Chris Keryokis asked merrily, "All of you are grandparents, but I'm not. Does being Debbie's godfather give me any status?"

"You're the leavening in the bread," Tim assured him. "When we go off the deep end, you can put us back on target because you're not emotionally involved. O.K.?"

As far as I was concerned, it was not O.K. It was wonderful! It was an intelligent group, a highly qualified grandparent group, and one which had never embraced the customary sex-caste system in which men talk shop in one corner of the room and ladies talk house in the other. I knew I could count on a lively, first-hand exchange that might clue me in to some of the reactions that would be forthcoming when my book was published. I knew also that no conversions either way would take place—if only because few opinionated human beings (and aren't we all?) stop to distinguish between steadfastness and stubbornness. Rarely, if ever, do we pause intelligently on our own to find that unmarked place where praiseworthy perseverance ends and stupid pigheadedness begins. Mostly, instead, we turn our little daily lives into one big Roman Arena, ready, almost, to die at the drop of one small conviction, lest any of our ideas perish from this earth; sticking to them all fanatically, the same senseless, cohesive way that vulcanized patches stick to an inner tube!

This being inherent human nature, however, I not only was prepared for what followed, but sat back happily to listen.

"Let's begin with the baby-sitting business." Fred, as usual, was the self-appointed chairman. "Did you cover that, Edwina?"

"Would it be a book about grandparenting if I didn't?" I answered.

Everyone laughed appreciatively. Then Chris asked, "This is my opportunity to ask something I've wondered about for a long time. Why do you let yourselves get imposed on so much? You're not old enough to sit in a heap by the fire. Getting out matters—so why do you do it?"

"I don't do it," Hilda protested.

"Well, I do," Gwen Richards declared defensively.

"Because it's the only time you get to see your grandchildren," her husband reminded her. "Or your children, either."

"I know," she admitted. "By baby-sitting, I feel I'm less of a stranger to the little ones. They can be a drain, though. I guess I'm not as young as I used to be."

Sympathetic noises filled the room.

Janet Scott spoke up next. "I really love my grandchildren," she said, "and I like being with them. But they do wear me out. And I guess I'm not too much at ease with

161

them. Somehow, I can't get too close."

"It's our daughter-in-law," Stewart Scott explained. "That girl uses the children as a weapon when anything comes up. If she doesn't like something Janet says or does, then she won't let the children visit."

More sympathetic noises filled the room.

"Personally," Christine Shultz made her contribution hesitantly, "I baby-sit because I don't want to tangle with my children—you know what I mean: I don't want them to get angry."

"I know just what you mean," Janet exclaimed.

"So do I," admitted Hilda. "Sure, I don't baby-sit, but it's cost me. There is a real gap. And I'm always trying to make up for it by buying them things. I never go to any of their houses empty-handed."

As Hilda spoke, I realized suddenly that this was an absolute truth for me, too. Whenever Tim and I went over to Debbie's, we carried burnt offerings for Melinda: A little dress, a doll, a toy, a book.

"Good Lord, Hilda," I said excitedly; "I never thought about it until just now. The stores are full of grandmothers buying baby things for their grandchildren. I almost wouldn't dare show up at Debbie's without a present. Why?"

We went off on this tangent for a little while. The consensus seemed to be that grandparents, because of their insecurity in their relationship with their grandchildren, bring presents as a means of currying favor. Gifts and the expectation of gifts surrounded the grandparents with importance in the eyes of the grandchildren. Notice of a visiting grandparent was thus ensured, and risk of hurt from being ignored was also, in this way, usually avoided.

"Do the youngsters sense what's happening?" Tim asked next. "Do you think they see through it all?"

Again, we went off on a tangent and again, there was more or less agreement—except for Janet Scott, who was sure children nowadays were smarter than any previous generation of children had ever been. The rest of the group, however, attributed most of the current childhood brilliance to a combination of mimicry and smart-aleckyness, so that there was an overall acceptance of the idea that the grandchildren merely accept the gifts as their due, while their parents look upon the whole performance as conduct befitting doting grandparents.

It comforted me, as I listened, to hear this unsolicited confirmation of my own personal conviction that the current crop of kids is not composed of intellectual Supermen. As far as I could ever see, most youngsters are notoriously like little chameleons. They are quick and gifted at taking on the characteristics of the background and people with which and whom they live until they emerge like walking, talking caricatures of their parents or teachers or friends. And all of this, of course, is enhanced by the constant exposure to the full range of modern television, and by a social climate that encourages children to be fully seen and freely heard, with scarcely any remaining barriers or formal restraints between the generations!

Thus, in general, an actor's son is often stage-struck while still in diapers; a plumber's son is usually a good one to have around to handle a leak; and I, myself, was camp counsellor once to an undertaker's daughter, who was as much at home among the corpses (particularly the baby ones, she said) as the rest of her ten-year-old compatriots were among their dolls. All of these little ones, moreover, are capable—in their fields—of impressive technical recitations, which invariably arouse adult astonishment and over-appreciation as if there were a sudden awareness that it is a pinafored child behind the wheel of a passing, interstate van instead of a truckdriver.

Hilda summed up this aspect of our discussion in her usual blunt way. "Our grandchildren are cute and endearing. So are puppies. Are they extra bright and extra beautiful? Probably not—even though their parents expect us to act as if they were. For myself, though, I can't take on in that fashion because I've lived long enough to see too many marvelous, gorgeous babies grow up into ordinary human beings."

At this point, I stood up to pass the bowl of nuts, but my ears were glued to Tim's next contribution.

"Hilda," he said slowly, "you've just touched on something that has been my own pet peeve. Why do our children expect us to go ape over their children? Why are grandparents supposed to be overcome with awe by their grandchildren? Don't our sons and daughters realize that we've been down the same road that they're on now? That we can love their little ones, but that we don't have to be dumbfounded by the wondrous phenomenon?"

"You're one hundred percent right!" Christine explained, the moment Tim stopped speaking. "And I'll tell you something else: it ties right in with that baby-sitting business we were talking about before. My daughter honestly believes that I must be delighted to be given the privilege of baby-sitting her children. She is allowing me to have her precious possessions for a little while. I love those kids—I really do—almost the way I loved my own when they were small. But I still don't feel overjoyed, because I'm going to get a chance to be with them at a time when it's convenient for her, but inconvenient for me. And she doesn't understand. So I just go into my act whenever she says the word, and pretend that there's nothing in the world I want more than a chance to get a first-hand look at a live baby and a dirty diaper—something I've never been blessed with in my whole life before!"

We all smiled at Christine. Fred reached for her hand as he said, "She's just chicken. She's scared her precious children will get mad at her. Right, honey?"

"Get mad at her?" Chris repeated with obvious curiosity. "You know, I've been struck in all this talk with one main thing. All of you seem almost frightened to be direct and frank at your dealings with your children in their role as parents. What's that all about anyway?"

164

For a moment, there was silence.

Then Janet said, "But you don't understand, Chris. It's not easy to communicate with grown children. They think we're criticizing or interfering in their lives. They're so touchy."

"All kinds of things creep in." Harry Richards picked up the threads in his slow, careful way. "They're your children and yet they're not your children. Take the whole money bit. Where grown children are concerned, it's more than the root of evil. It's the evil itself."

"You can bet your last dollar on that!" Fred could scarcely contain himself. "Most of us here made it the hard way to our present comfortable economic status. It took years and years of hard work and careful planning and lots of doing without in the beginning. But our kids want it all right now. They see what we've got, and they're not prepared to wait out their time to get it on their own."

It was Hilda, surprisingly, who rose to a defense.

"And why should they be prepared to wait it out?" she demanded. "Before they go off on their own, we share our goodies with them. Suddenly, at a given point, we shut them off from the Fountain of Comparative Wealth. And when they settle down and have children of their own, they want· to set a right proper style of living—even if they can't afford it—just like Mom and Dad."

"Exactly," agreed Fred. "So they expect help all the way, and whatever you give never seems enough."

"Which breeds resentfulness and bad feelings." Christine, the psychologist, stood staunchly beside her husband. "The whole system is off balance, if you ask me. They don't want us meddling; they pride themselves on their independence. But how independent are you when you have to ask your parents for the down payment on a house? And how can you keep from seeming meddlesome when you want to know What and Why in response to a request for money?"

There was a distinct murmur of affirmation to Christine's rhetorical question. Then Janet asked, almost wistfully,

"But how can you *not* help them when they need it?" to which Hilda answered, without a moment's hesitation, "You can't."

"And that," finished Christine emphatically, "is a good part of the uneasiness that causes so many family problems. You help because you'd feel guilty if you didn't. They take it because they need it or want it and you have it—but they hate the whole idea. In the end, it's you who are held responsible for their own inadequacies, and they wind up ready at the drop of a hat to go off in a huff."

The moment Christine said "huff," Chris returned to his original observation and enlarged upon it.

"I really would like to know just what it is that keeps you all so tense in your dealings with your children and your grandchildren," he repeated. "What if they do get annoyed with you at times? Would that stop their being your children again the next day?"

Would it? I thought about it for a long, sober moment. Could my Debbie, whom we had loved and raised for all of her life and the greater part of our lives, ever turn away from her father and me? Was such a terrible thing even a remote possibility?

Before I could resolve this issue to my own private satisfaction, Tim spoke up. "It's funny, Chris," he said, "that you should say that today. Just yesterday, I was drawing up a will for an old client of mine—a family whose legal affairs I've handled for several years. The man wanted to know if you had to disinherit a son specifically in a will, or was it enough merely not to mention him. I knew he had a daughter—an only child, I'd thought—and I asked him why he wanted to know. Turns out he also has a son in Philadelphia whom he and his wife haven't heard from in twenty-two years. They had a disagreement way back then and that was the end of the relationship."

"How awful!"

"It's incredible!"

"It must be a most unusual case!"

These comments around the room came to an abrupt halt as Gwen Richards' voice rose above the rest, "It's not unusual. It happens." She stopped, obviously embarrassed, then decided to plunge on. "Harry and I don't like to talk about this, you know, but we haven't seen Margie in almost a year."

Her voice broke as she turned her face away and hid it against Harry's shoulder. He continued for her. "I know you've all heard about Margie's divorce and remarriage. Well, when we first learned what was happening, we went all out to try to make Margie hold her marriage together for the sake of her three little children, at least. She was so angry because we wouldn't back her up—not that Tom, her ex-husband was any objectionable kind of a guy—that she stopped talking to us for the most part. Then, when she remarried six months later, she told us we couldn't come to her house at all because her new husband didn't want us. He thought we hadn't been warm enough towards him and she said she didn't want to argue the point with him. Just like that."

"Just like that!" Hilda's voice had a disbelieving sound.

We all had known Harry and Gwen for many years. We had watched Margie grow up; we had attended her first wedding; we had followed the birth of each of her babies; we had seen the closeness, the concern that had existed between her parents and her; we had gossiped—but not with malice—about the lavishness and endlessness of the gifts with which they had endowed her and her family; we had even occasionally envied the warmth and solidity of their relationship. And now this—how could one clash wipe out everything that had gone before?

As Gwen sat up again, dabbing at her eyes, Tim broke the stunned silence and said sympathetically, "We had no idea at all, Gwen, of what you and Harry have been going through. But maybe things will improve before too long, and you and Margie can get together again the way you used to."

"I doubt it," Gwen answered sadly. "We don't see her. She calls once every three or four weeks and it hurts because she sounds like a stranger. And I'm sure I sound like a stranger to her. We're stiff and formal and her children are the same way. They don't know me anymore and I don't know them. "She stopped speaking for a moment. Then she cleared her throat and went on in a firmer voice. "Look here," she said, trying to laugh about it, "I only went into this to make you see that these things can happen anywhere. Sure, we're insecure where our children are concerned. Probably, way down deep, we know that we can't count on them for anything, especially their love. We would never cut them out of our lives because they are our lives. But they're capable of walking away from us because we represent a part of their lives that has ended. They've got new fish to fry and they don't need us to help fry them."

No one, apparently, was disposed to argue this point or, for that matter, to openly acknowledge it. Instead, the next question surfaced in the course of some general, noncommittal remarks. Had it been this same way, we all wondered aloud, between our parents and ourselves?

"I was a maverick," Hilda announced promptly. "Not that I wanted to horrify my mother, but we were further apart than Alaska and Guam. Every time she would visit me after I was married, you could tell that she thought our apartment looked like an outhouse and that I was dressed like Dracula."

"And she would glance at me," Larry added gaily, "as if to check on skeletal disintegration because I was living on Hilda's cooking."

When we finished laughing, Janet conceded that she and her mother had similar problems. For Janet's mother, apparently, the path to heaven was paved with spic and span, and the road to Hell was waylaid by tattletale gray. The daily battles she waged in the glorified names of cleanliness and propriety would have made the whole Korean and Viet

168

Nam messes, rolled together, seem as casual as a game of cops and robbers.

"My mother didn't want me to marry Fred," Christine volunteered next. "I was supposed to have a fabulous career until about thirty, at which time I was to make a match that would put Grace Kelly's to shame. And what did I do but take up at nineteen with a penniless law student!"

"Harry's mother was almost as bad," laughed Gwen. "She has never really forgiven her son, the Doctor, for settling on a poor little nurse. And the fact that I was an orphan was another serious affront! She used to go on and on about my having no 'proper family' and there was always the veiled implication that I must have killed them off myself!"

There was another burst of laughter at this, and then a sudden silence. You could almost hear the wheels spinning as the realization swept over all of us: it had indeed been very much the same way with our parents and ourselves!

"But it was a more controlled kind of thing," Fred finally decided, as if we had spoken aloud. "They complained about us and we let them. It was like playing Monopoly. We all knew the rules of the game. They couldn't make us adhere to their concept of life and we couldn't make them like ours. But it never turned into a hand-to-hand combat for survival."

"And with few exceptions," Gwen said, with just a shade of bitterness, "we would never dream of saying, 'Don't darken my door anymore.' No matter what they said or did, they were our mothers and fathers. That meant a great deal." ❦

"And no matter what we said or did," Hilda completed the thought, "we were their children. They were the ones who would always stand by, the ones we could always turn to when the chips were down. There was a bond there that nothing and no one could ever break."

"So," Fred began his summation, "it was the same and yet it wasn't. There was a loyalty between our parents and us that gave both generations a sense of security. They didn't have to worry that we would get angry and have nothing more to do with them—at least, on the whole—and that sureness on their part extended down to the grandchildren. They were at ease with them for the same reasons. They didn't have to curry favor or importance by gift giving and sweet talk."

"Are you saying then," asked Tim, "that the major difference between how it was and how it is, is that we're just plain afraid? Afraid our children will turn on us for keeps."

"Essentially," Fred answered. "You've heard the girls talking. They didn't please their mothers either. We all went our own way and did our own thing. But family breaches were comparatively rare and now they're more common. And knowing this, we all walk on nails when we approach our youngsters. After all the time and love and effort—yes, and even money—that we've invested in our children, we don't dare to speak or act frankly for fear of alienating them—and with them, our grandchildren."

It was a sobering thought for me, if only because I had never expressed it even secretly in so blunt a way. It was obviously a sobering thought for everyone else, too.

"I guess you're right," Hilda finally said, "although I can think of at least one instance where the relationship between the parents and children and grandchildren is just perfect. My daughter-in-law, as a matter of fact. She and her mother and father are really good and close friends. It's beautiful, the easy give and take that they have between them."

"Oh, there are exceptions," Fred conceded. "But not too many. And anyway," he added, laughing, "we can always hope that things will get better as all of us—including the kids—get older. Right?"

The party ended on this tinge of optimism. It was getting late by then and everyone was ready to go. For myself, however, as usual, the silent reflections went on and on.

I thought back over my own personal adjustments since Melinda had been born. I thought also of the stresses and

170

strains we had all endured separately and together. I thought finally of that first, original question that had launched the entire discussion for the evening, "But what does it all mean?" And I realized regretfully that I still didn't know.

Maybe, I postulated to myself, there is never any understanding it in any case. Maybe the most that one can hope for is a graceful acceptance of the whole grandparental role which is as much parental as it is anything else. Maybe that was all our parents, in their turn, had ever achieved when they bore with much the same kind of brazen disregard and self-concern that we manifested when our children were small. And maybe, in the end, there is a long-range, overall justice in the process that produces a true balance of mental and emotional growth in life—because in this way and in due season, we are guaranteed an ever-changing dose of everything: We are the frustraters, then the frustrated; the joyous, then the despairing; the leaders, then the led; the doers, then the undone; the parents, then the Grandparents.

Somehow, this private analysis gave me a feeling of comparative peace that seemed to take the last edge off my grandparental adjustment. I sensed it even before I fell asleep that night, and I knew it for sure the next day when Debbie and Pete stopped by in the afternoon to make an announcement.

"Mother and Daddy," she said with an air of self-importance and with her hand in Pete's, "we just wanted to tell you now—we were going to before, when Melinda got sick: Well, we're going to have another baby. In five months."

In the congratulatory flurry which followed—and this time, Tim and I went through all the proper motions—I could not help thinking how far in this grandparent business I had come. I was neither overly impressed nor unduly depressed, but merely matter of fact about all that lay ahead. And this reaction to the imminence of a second grandchild, I realized, was the ultimate and truest test of one's adjustment to grandparenthood as a way of life.

As I kissed Debbie and hugged Pete and wished them well, I knew beyond any reasonable doubt that I was a full-fledged grandma at last.

LISETTE
By Patricia Ann Rob

PRICE: $2.25 LB745
CATEGORY: Historical Romance

Lisette, daughter of a murdered French Marquis, and her twin brother flee from her father's castle with family jewels they plan to deliver to their grandfather in Scotland. They are pursued across France and England by a man who wants the priceless jewels for himself. Lisette is seduced by the Duke of Melton, and then runs away. Realizing his love for her is genuine, the Duke launches a search that rescues her from a terrible fate, and they are reunited in love.

BRIDE OF THE ROLLING PLAINS
Jean Haught

PRICE: $2.25 LB753
CATEGORY: Historical Romance (Original)

When Rebecca Pearson first met handsome Steve
Mourgan, a scout for the wagon train bearing her
westward, she fell instantly in love. Joined by
passion yet separated by disaster, they vowed to
overcome the barriers that kept them apart!

IN LOVE AND WAR
By Lorinda Hagen

PRICE: $2.25 LB719
CATEGORY: Novel (Original)

Esther, a minister's daughter from a small town, goes to Cincinnati to seek her fortune. She is discovered singing in a night club and is signed for a national tour and an opportunity for a movie test. She meets Neil Patterson, an aspiring novelist, who sells his first book to Hollywood. Esther gets the lead in his film at Neil's insistence. Esther Eden becomes a star and marries Neil. But they are soon separated when Neil signs on as a war correspondent after the attack on Pearl Harbor. Their world is torn apart, not only by the war, but by rumors of Esther's infidelity. Esther wages a passionate battle to hold onto the only man she has ever really loved.

MOTHERS AND LOVERS
By Jeannie Sakol
Best selling author of "Hot 30" and "Flora Sweet"

PRICE: $2.25 LB743
CATEGORY: Novel

A witty, romantic novel of the intricate relationships between mother and daughter, husband and wife, man and woman. Stephanie, twenty-four, pregnant and on the verge of a divorce, blames her mother Melissa for the mess she's in. But Melissa's life has been no bed of roses either. Stephanie finally realizes that no one is responsible for another's mistakes. She must solve her own problems and fulfill her own destiny.